Also by
LLOYD HOLLIS CROOKS

Sister, Because of You

Blood on the Blade

Peeping Through the Keyhole

Ice and Eyes in the Sun: True Love Comes Late, Sometimes

Grenada Ghost

WHEN WISDOM WHISPERS

A Novel By

LLOYD HOLLIS CROOKS

WAYNE BRATHWAITE PUBLISHERS
www. lloydholliscrooks.com

Published 2020

Library of Congress Control No. 2019905746
ISBN 978-0-578-63413-5
Printed in the United States
Designed by: nkkoprinting@gmail.com

THIS BOOK IS IN LOVING MEMORY
OF, AND DEDICATED TO
MY DECEASED PARENTS:

Alister Lenard Brathwaite

Ruth Brathwaite

Joseph Sears

Leoni Crooks-Sears

Who showed me the way when I was lost at the cross roads.

ACKNOWLEDGMENTS

I strove with this novel, based on a true story that may make you cry in the end, to add a somewhat personal perspective of lovers' behavior knowing fully well my so-called fresh perspective may become a laughing stock in social media chatter. I had read in the past critics' sarcasms on another subject that I had ventured to add an opinion, and although their sarcasms were brutal, I enjoyed them to the hilt. I am an octogenarian, but I am minus hubris in love affairs. I am not a know-it-all about the varied experiences in one's love affairs—neither their triumphs nor heartbreaks. As an author, I try hard not to soak up and bundle the narratives of past events of jilted-love affairs confessed to me by the jilted ones who trusted my friendship and my own jilted heartbreaks when I had fallen in love for the first time at age nineteen with an East Indian girl thinking that would have been my first and last jilted love affair. I had other heartbreaks, too many, almost habitually.

In writing *When Wisdom Whispers* I purposely chose the journey of an 8-year-old girl named Dixie who once traversed Brooklyn streets with her mother, Florence, hungry and homeless, to when in older years Dixie fell in love, and life became kinder to her having the luxury of jubilating on satin sheets with her true love.

Nigel K.C. Crooks, I thank you very much for giving me the title for my book, *When Wisdom Whispers.* You told me your mother gave you the title in a dream. I hope what I have written pleases you, and your deceased mother, my wife, posthumously. Nigel, you will be surprised to know your wisdom shines in this novel. The advice Officer Kirl Cardus gives to Cocoa Panyol, a round character in the novel, who loses his lover in a vehicular accident and wants to commit suicide, are your words of advice: "It is the hard stuff that makes us what we are."

A.H. Rudberg, M.D., F.A.C.S., Diplomate of the American Board of Urology, I again thank you profusely from the bottom of my heart for your keen, medical attention to me from the year Two Thousand and One to today. You are responsible for a great part of my life before and after my prostate cancer procedure. You have a way of making me laugh out loud even when I am in pain. When you retire from your prolific, medical practice—and I hope not soon—please, do some moonlighting at Comedy Central in Manhattan. Smile. I also thank your amiable staff in the heart of Little Odessa, Brighton Beach, 231

Oceanview Avenue, Brooklyn, New York 11235, for their courtesy and attention to details about my sickness.

Dr. Rudberg, you will be surprised to know in your waiting room I have proofread and edited four of my books. I have six (6) books in print. Tell me what books you don't have, and I will be happy to give them for your bookshelf hoping you will read all of them.

I thank you very much, A'Ferti Ma'at Amun-Re-EL, Native American of Aniyunwiya (Cherokee), Miccouskee, Creek, Seminole, Washita and Yamassee descent. Because of you, my vacation in Citrus Springs, Florida, was grand. You were my tourist guide, *par excellence*. You made yourself my private chauffeur; you took me to Indian Mounds at Crystal River, related the Indian demise by the very people the Indians fed—those ungrateful expatriates—and when you prayed among those Mounds of your deceased Indian people, I was emotionally moved. Surely, I shall return to "drink deep" of your knowledge of Indian history and culture.

I thank you, Janice Longmore Owens, RN, and your beautiful daughter, Dominique Griffith, for your hospitality and accommodation in your beautiful home in Citrus Springs, Florida. I wrote the first chapter of my novel in your home. The taste of your nourishing Jamaican dishes on my palate was a plus to your many other kindnesses.

Seven-year-old Jaden "Major" Haye, I thank you very much for your amusement and for teaching me how to dance the floss when we shared company in the summer of 2018. When we sat in Baisley Pond Park, relaxed, and watched joggers go by, you said, "Mr. Crooks, even though you are my babysitter, I will tell people who ask, 'Who are you?' that you are my good friend. I will not tell them you are my babysitter." I was most surprised when I read your composition, A DAY WITH MR. CROOKS, in which you thanked me for taking care of you in the absence of your parents. Your composition is also pasted on my WALLS OF MEMORIES AND CHAMPIONS with my grand and great grandchildren's compositions.

Ashaki Cash Nehisi, you are the quintessential person to have in my corner: You are smart, reliable, self-contained, and a nerd then and now. I had a problem that the Cell Company that sold me my cell phone could not remedy, and you solved that problem in five minutes. At the age of eight, you were a chess champ in your division, and I look at your picture on my WALLS OF MEMORIES AND CHAMPIONS of you concentrating on your next chess move. You do the job given no matter what it costs to you—time or money. I knew you would not equivocate with an answer when I asked you to write the Foreword to my novel, *When Wisdom Whispers.* You answered, "Sure, Gramps!" I call you nearly every day to fix things, for social media help, for proofreading my text, and correcting my grammar. (What a difference time makes.) You are my secretary without portfolio. I am so happy to be your neighbor, and I am happier to be your Gramps because you watch over me.

Marie-Sophie Cornu, I thank you very much for translating my poem from English to French at such short notice, and for your lovely letters educating me of your famous homeland, France. I hope in writing other books, should I again need your translation help, I can call on you. Smile. Sunday, September 15, 2019, was a red-letter day for me. I had a wonderful time with you, Khafra, and Maia, my great granddaughter. We walked from your home in Bedford Stuyvesant to downtown Brooklyn, now known as SOMA (South of Manhattan), had lunch in a restaurant, and then we sat in the park, took pictures, and had a lovely outdoor in the cool of the evening.

Olivia, your twin brother Josiah, and Greyson Jackson, I thank you very much for welcoming me into your lovely home, for showing me around the North East, Maryland neighborhood, and for giving me the opportunity to edit my novel instead of babysitting you for the full time that your parents were at work.

Olivia, when you said, "Grandpa Crooks, I want to interview you," I asked you why. You said, "For posterity…I want to remember you when you are gone; I want to laugh when I am reading your jokes and quickly turning the pages of your novels; and especially to laugh out loud about your tales of your dangerous adventures in your upbringing in The Republic of Trinidad and Tobago. And last, but not least, for making palatable breakfasts for us, whom you call "The 3Ts," every morning before we go to school. Your life is a tale of many circumstances."

Olivia, Josiah, and Greyson, your interview now makes my hereafter, which I once called fiction, a reality in fact, because my name and events of what I did in my lifetime will be on your lips when I'm dust. I also thank your parents, Trish-Ellen and Curtis Jackson, for their generous hospitality whenever I am in their home.

I also have overwhelming gratitude for my dear friend, Georgia Haye. I thank you, Georgia, very much for your friendship throughout the years, and for your words of advice that have helped me in times of difficulty. You have never demurred on giving me your view points on politics, religion, family, love and its heartaches, name it.

I will never forget your caregiving patience when you took care of my sick wife who has since passed away. May God's grace, strength, and wisdom, be with you as you navigate your life during your "pensionable" years. Thank you will never be enough, but THANK YOU and your husband Winston, anyway.

I am nothing without my children. My seven children may not know that my life has been a trying and difficulty journey; but seeing your successes I rise every morning with joy thinking of you and your future. I trust that your help when I'm no longer lucid would be evident for it will be given with love and affection. You know I love to be alone, and your stay should be short when you visit. You always call me to know how am I, only to receive my patented, "I'm okay, very okay." Thanks a million for your love which I reciprocate ten-fold.

It gives me great pleasure to thank you again, Dr. Patricia E.D. Belcon, Socio-Carnivalist, and joint Author-Editor of *Re-Igniting The Ancestral Fires: Heritage, Traditions, And Legacies of the First Peoples.* In all my novels and true stories, I apply in my texts the knowledgeable resources of sociology you painstakingly imparted to us, your students, at Medgar Evers College.

Finally, because of COVID-19 I delayed

publishing my novel, WHEN WISDOM WHISPERS. My spare time was mountain high and Ezlon Crooks, an ex-Veteran, who works at James A. H Haley Veterans' Hospital, in Tampa, Florida, said, "Dad, why not join The Literature Group (TLG) chat. I am the Moderator. We can even discuss your new novel, WHEN WISDOM WHISPERS." I mumbled words without meaning. Then he quoted Judy Garland's: "When you get to know a lot of people, you make a great discovery." Two days later I joined TLG.

The Group's members live on the Continent of Africa, in the United States, in the United Kingdom, and in the Caribbean. Many times our discussions went from one day into the other nonstop. Our topics were varied: conflicts in relationships—marrying out of your race; slavery—it's time to move on (the exchanges were for and against); the institutions of socialization—religion, politics, family, education, economics; COVID-19 pandemic; fashions; singing and songs. The older members prefer standards sung by Frank Sinatra, Tony Bennett, Ella Fitzgerald, and others performers of their time whom they said their phrasings in their songs were immaculate; a young member of TLG sang in a video, and she welcomed our praises for her voice and personality. The topics aforementioned are just a few. Nevertheless, our topic always ended on the tidal wave of joblessness the world over because of COVID-19, wondering where the virus truly originated, and who in governments knew of the approaching Coronavirus pandemic and kept quiet because of politics.

The clarion call for TLG discussions was about a white Minneapolis Police Officer Derek Chauvin, casually with one hand in his pocket, who put his knee on George Floyd's neck for 8 minutes and 46 seconds and killed him.

On May 6, 2020, Yaundeen Wright, a scholar, an "imaginative poet who has masterfully fused the sacred with the profane" joined TLG. She read an excerpt of Stereotype, a poem, which to me, delves into Gender and Identity, from her book, *Teachers Are Human Too*. She told TLG tidbits of her background and said, "I don't aspire to be an ivory tower writer; I aspire to make a difference." Wright was heartily welcomed by The Literature Group.

I bought Wright's Teachers Are Human Too. I asked Cash Nehisi, my granddaughter, to introduce herself to TLG and read Wright's Stereotype. She did; and members of TLG were impressed with her diction and style, especially when she read Wright's words of women who enter the marriage graveyard, et al: I AM NOT ONE OF THOSE WOMEN. "Those women" arched in Nehisi's voice as just pastoral folks, even less than.

Teachers Are Human Too should be on the Great White Way—Broadway.

Thus, it gives me great pleasure to name the members of TLG. They made my sadness because of COVID-19 lessen considerably, and Judy Garland's words became alive by my joining The Literature Group.

The names of members of TLG who made my days happy while the Coronavirus pandemic was raging in the United States are: Ezlon Crooks, nicknamed Navy Man, Founder and Moderator; Victoria Catherine Brathwaite; Stacy Herbert; Brianna Monique Kayla Kiki Crooks; Loveth Idehen; Kamille Harris; Lois Eva Wilson; Hilton Thomas; Janice Longmore-Owens; Anitra Lampkin; Yaundeen Wright; and Linda Kelly Richards.

The women were alpha females. They *ad lib* similes and metaphors in split seconds to prove their points especially when Ezlon Crooks teased them as if their knowledge in science, medicine, and the humanities is less than men's; none is my favorite in language or the vernacular; but when Ezlon Crooks put forward an opinion that grated Stacy Herbert's dentures, her soft voice became an ambulance siren, "Navy Man! Everybody has an opinion and an anus."

I told Herbert I am going to plagiarize her

truth and put it in my novel. She said laughing aloud, her laughter echoed in my cell phone, "Mr. Crooks, it's now yours."

"Thank you, Ms. Herbert, for giving me such words of wisdom."

"You are welcome, Mr. Crooks."

The day and night became one.

We continued the chat for months.

I am looking at the morning's sun through
my window
She shines for all of us—the just and the unjust
No matter the conditions of life
Stay focused my people.

Faye Longmore

"Don't envy me for the seeds that I have sown; envy me for the harvest I reap."
Ruby Adassa Stewart says she heard those words many years ago, and she memorized them to tell me.

Bitterness does not keep you warm.

Stacy Herbert.

What tastes good in your mouth, sometimes tastes bitter in your behind, boy.

Leoni Crooks-Sears
(My Mother)

FOREWORD

If there's one, true reason why I said yes to write the Foreword for the novel, *When Wisdom Whispers*, based on a true story, and written by Lloyd Hollis Crooks, it is the fact that the author, my grandfather, whom I call Gramps, corrected my grammar when I was a teenager; and, more important, he fills the role of a sage elder.

Lest I forget, he does not like gifts or to speak of his accomplishments.

A novel with a deeply pertinent analysis of love affairs, of heartbreaks, of struggles, of dreams, of tragedy, and of present-day American politics is *When Wisdom Whispers.* I am warning you the ending may be tearful for you.

It is the journey of black, 8-year-old Dixie Dunkirk, hungry, traversing Brooklyn streets with her mother, Florence, holding her hand. Both were looking for a place to call home after being evicted by the landlord for their continuous late and non-payments of rents because of their poverty. Every cloud has a silver lining, and the silver lining in that cloud of their lives is a black-5-year-old boy, named Jason, riding his bicycle in a predominantly white neighborhood. Jason hears Dixie's cry for help and answers: "Ask Aunt Ruby. She helps everybody."

Aunt Ruby is the Good Samaritan, a round character, and a true person who at times relates the story.

Years rolled on. Forty-year-old Dunkirk became happy, enjoying her life to the hilt, choosing men of her exquisite taste, falling in love with Jason, gives him her O-negative blood to save his life, then dumping him; but her final choice shocked Aunt Ruby to the core.

Crooks, whose life is unlike any of Horatio Alger's characters in his story about impoverished boys and their lives from humble backgrounds to lives of middle-class security and comfort, came into this Diaspora from being a Confidential Secretary in Whitehall, in the Prime Minister's Office, the seat of Government, in the Republic of Trinidad and Tobago (T&). In T&T, he covered "sensitive" National and International Conferences.

His writing style crafts a layered, colorful perspective of love, of duty, and of the ties that bind for characters whose stories are both familiar and surprising. Through his words, the culture and the diversity of Queens, which has the most naturalized immigrant population in New York, come alive: lovers unite, lovers break up, heartbreak surfaces, loyalties to the characters shifts, and everyone has a story to tell—sometimes bitter, sometimes bitter-sweet, and sometimes truly sweet because forgiveness prevails in the heart of the jilted lover.

When Wisdom Whispers is tantamount to tracing the threads of a patchwork quilt. We weave in and out of the characters' lives, slowly connecting the tender and tumultuous moments, to ultimately take a step back in view of how relationships sometimes fall together and fall apart. Crooks's text delves into that institution of socialization called "Family," and the adjustments members of a family make before settling down, and burying their sharp hatchets and deep grudges. Ultimately, the journey of Dixie Dunkirk creates a memorable project filled with 'ole-time' Caribbean proverbs, with heartache, with humor, triumphs and tragedy, and with sharp-tongued dialogues that only Crooks could stitch together because of his past travels when he left his homeland and his present experiences in this Diaspora.

This novel explores the ups and downs

of loving another through their relationship. It is an honest portrayal of what happens after the initial butterflies and fluttering eyelashes. What does love look like the second time around? What does it look like after that?

The author has a unique ability to jump into the lives of his characters, as if he is they, and anchors their personalities in such a way that we can all relate to in some degree. The dialogues encompass politics, comedy, sex—who is the better soloist below the belly button where it is dark—and reminders of self-preservation. I hear my grandmother's echo in Dixie's cheeky remarks. I see my taciturn grandfather's watchful eyes in how Darwin stares the immigrant joggers in their panty-shorts on their moving derrieres in Baisley Pond Park. I recognize my aunt's sharp tongue in Eldika Wolmers' audacious responses to her father, Darwin. Eldika and Darwin are also round characters in this novel, and their guile is thick and dirtier than red mud.

You will laugh out loud; you will gasp clutching your pearls; and you will learn about love: how it endures, how it ebbs and flows, how it sometimes comes rushing in and leaves all at once. Whether it is the familial love that makes space for a homeless child as Dixie Dunkirk or the romantic love of the said Dunkirk that inspires a leap of faith; all of the meanderings of her journey will pucker up as you anxiously turn the pages of *When Wisdom Whispers*.

In this love story Crooks is perforced to write of the racist remarks of the bafflegab President a.k.a. Individual One, Radicalizer in Chief, Liar-Above-All and Minus One brandishing prejudice as patriotism. There he is shouting to four Black Americans Congresswomen "go back to where you came from." Individual One's racism is mellifluous, but most pleasant in the ears of his fans, his kith and kin, whose hatred of black and brown peoples is deep, forgetting they, the Mayflower descendants, are the true expatriates.

Here's hoping you will not blame the author for how his novel ends—I almost did. You and I will only blame Crooks if we did not all lean in and listen to when wisdom whispers in this human story.

Ashaki Cash Nehisi

CHAPTER 1

Darwin Wolmers had gotten up 3 A.M. on May 19, 2018, and turned on CNN to view the wedding with its pomp and pageantry of Prince Harry and Meghan Markle. May 19 was also his daughter, Eldika's birthday. She was fourteen years old, precocious, extremely inquisitive, and conversant with social media chatter. Darwin had woken her up because she had told him she's interested in seeing the wedding and all the ceremonies that followed. Father and daughter sat in their favorite, damaged, and patched leather couch; they hit each other's knees playfully, and listened with rapt attention to Bishop Michael Bruce's 13-minute address and advice to Prince Harry and Meghan Markle, the Duke and Duchess of Sussex, in which the Bishop spoke of the redemptive power of love specifically to the bride and bridegroom.

The bride and bridegroom's faces beamed

with love and affection for each other.

"Eldie, how do you like the ceremony and Bishop Bruce's advice to the bride and bridegroom?"

"The wedding ceremony was okay, daddy. But I didn't understand what the Bishop meant with all those big words."

"What big words? At your age you should know the meaning of every word the Bishop said." She did not answer.

"Did you look at the face of Queen Elizabeth, the grandmother of Harry, and also at the face of Miss Ragland, the mother of Meghan?"

"The Queen had a deceitful, half smile on her face, exactly as yours, when you don't want to increase my allowance, saying you are broke, and you have no money in Chase Bank where you work. Miss Ragland had a sweet smile on her face because she was happy to see her beautiful daughter, Meghan, got married to a rich man; and she would not have to beg for an allowance as often as I beg you because her daughter will give her plenty money to put in her purse to go shopping in the big stores that are near to her daughter's palace."

Eldie pulled the string on her pajamas, tightened the waist, looked her father in his eyes, and said, "Daddy, do you want to hear what Wendy's mother says what would happen to their marriage life because Harry is white and Meghan is brown?"

"Brown?" He stared into her eyes. "Meghan Markle is not black as the pot in the kitchen; but with one drop of black blood in your body you are black, and the Duchess has plenty drops."

"Since in kindergarten my teacher said a girl with Meghan's color is not black; she's brown."

"You have left kindergarten many years ago, and you know how I feel about giving black people another color."

"Daddy, your old-time thinking is not my new-time thinking. Why are you looking at me and not saying a word? Do you want to hear what Wendy's mother says, or not?"

"I don't want to hear, Eldie."

"I'm going back to sleep, but when I wake up I will still tell you what she says even if you don't want to hear."

"I don't want to hear. By the way, where does that woman get her information?"

"From the Lady Pope on daylight TV who knows everybody's business."

"Who the hell is she, Eldie? And when do you get the time to listen to the Lady Pope on daylight TV because I send you to school every day? Do you return to the house when I leave for work?"

"I will tell you that, too, if you make my breakfast before you go to Baisley Pond Park to listen to people's business as if you are working for the newspapers." She pulled the full sheet over her face and body.

An opinion on CNN is heard: The anchor says to his co-anchor, "Oprah Winfrey didn't like the first dress for Harry and Meghan's wedding, so she got another dress made for her overnight." The co-anchor replied, "Billionaire Oprah gets what billionaire Oprah wants."

Darwin smiled at their comments, took off the television, resumed his thoughts, reflected on his plan for the day, and mumbled to himself on his way to Baisley Pond Park: "The judge was fair. He gave me full custody of Eldie since she was three months old because my wife had a child for another man while I was in the Army. Now that I am out of the Army, I hope a good woman will come my way and be kind to my child." He laughed aloud, then said, comically, "#MeToo people in your #MeToo Movements, I have been following all of your rules for the good of womankind, and I hope this time I will get an obedient woman to be my wife." He paused. "Oh my god! I am sorry, #MeToo people, not an obedient woman, but a truthful and kind woman to be my future wife who will love my daughter. #MeToo people, let me be fair: I have plenty faults. I, too, was promiscuous in my marriage, but I do not have a child out of wedlock."

Darwin and his daughter live in South Jamaica, Queens, New York, on 155th Street, next to Winston and Georgia Haye, a beautiful family; and Winston beautifies the block in spring and summer with a variety of flowers, and he shovels his and his neighbors' snow in winter. Their grandson, Jaden Haye, nicknamed Major, seven years old, is a gifted comedian and dancer of hip-hop and pop music, and he lives with his grandparents.

On the edge of Baisley Pond Park where the pond juts out, passersby pelt pebbles to see the waves most times blocked by the lilies in bloom. Darwin loves to boast to his Brooklyn friends saying Baisley Pond Park is a most beautiful public park, and it contains over one hundred acres including thirty acres of the pond, and he goes fishing for largemouth bass in the pond. He always begins his boast in their presence:

"Let me tell you, dumb Brooklynites, especially those of you who live in dirty Flatbush and put out your garbage in brown paper bags because you are too cheap to buy authentic garbage bags, this park is a beloved institution for the neighborhood. Here we have concerts, festivals, weddings, parties, shows, reunions, sports, tennis, handball, basketball, cricket, and people go jogging, biking, and rollerblading; and in the summer the shady alcoves for barbecuing is there at our command. But, dumb Brooklynites, I don't mind having a woman from your noisy Brooklyn with the looks and shape of Cardi B." He laughs mockingly when he drops that desire on his Brooklyn friends who reply in unison, "No Brooklyn woman wants you, Darwin; you are too fuckin cheap and stingy; and you are dumber than we are because Cardi B with her obscenity in her music wouldn't be our decent people's choice."

Darwin walked down the incline by his house straight to the glass cage on display and read the information framed and wrote it in his notebook: Wet plants play an important role in supporting a variety of pond life, such as turtle, and fish, by reducing pollutants and by combining nutrients, carbon dioxide, water and sunlight to create oxygen and food. He stopped reading, rushed and sat on a bench, as a woman traveling recklessly on a golf cart came his way and beckoned to him to look at what is taking place in the park. She eased off her cart, sat next to him on his favorite, green bench, and said, "I know birds do it, but I didn't know those two do it, too."

Both watched as a tomcat invited a squirrel to play hide-and-seek around the trunk of a large birch tree next to the tennis court on the undulating ground of green grass.

"What do you think of them, fella?" The woman eased herself and her golf- cart closer to Darwin.

"They're probably showing us, humans, how to get along," Darwin answered.

"What you think they'd be saying about us, humans?"

"That you, on wheels, are not free as they are."

"Why should they be concentrating on

me, on wheels, and not you, barefooted walking on countless joggers' spit in this park?"

It was as if the squirrel, the innocent prey-to-be, and the big, black tomcat, the deceitful prowler, read Darwin and the woman's minds. They continued their peeping at each other similar to the way new lovers make their first approach to court a lover. The tomcat—let's call him Tom—made two steps backward and the squirrel—let's call her Betsy—made one step forward.

"See?" the woman said, and pulled her golf cart much closer to her body as if she felt Tom and Betsy may play hide-and-seek around her golf cart.

"See what?" Darwin asked.

"That romantic move."

"Whose romantic move?"

"The woman's."

"All I see is Tom thinking of a scheme to eat trusting Betsy. Women always trust men in a minute. I don't know why."

"If I, a woman, make a move as Tom's and

move closer to you, you'd eat me, ravenously?"

Darwin closed his notebook. He stopped writing the literature of Baisley Pond Park. His poker face was visible. "What's your name?"

"Why are you asking for my name?"

"I think I saw your face in Brooklyn before, and you were using your legs, not a golf cart."

"You are that observant about men's movements and whereabouts, too?"

Darwin didn't answer.

"My name is Dixie Dunkirk. When you saw me in Brooklyn, I hadn't an accident. Does that cover your curiosity? What's your name?"

"Darwin Wolmers. I come barefooted to the park every day because I love to feel the warmth of the asphalt and loose dirt on my soles."

"Don't you have a job?"

"I'm retired."

"So young?"

"I'm fifty five. I took early retirement, but I work part-time."

"Don't you want a full-time moonlighting job?"

"Doing what?"

"Pushing me?"

"When?"

"When my wheels are clogged, and they become difficult to climb the inclines in Baisley Pond Park."

Before Darwin could answer, Betsy made two steps backward away from the tree, and Tom made one step forward.

Dixie said, "See?"

Darwin said, "See what?"

"The woman's move is so romantic."

"As yours?"

"You think so, Darwin?"

"Let's change the subject."

"Are you antisocial, Mr. Wolmers?"

Seeing Darwin's blank face, Dixie drove away without saying goodbye, and Darwin went back writing about the beauty of Baisley Pond Park. But then he noticed Betsy sensed Tom was not a lover, and if she went closer to Tom, his teeth would be in her tender body.

That's when wisdom whispered in Betsy's ear. She hurried away, climbed up quickly on another tree, and branched off many other trees, as Tom hid in lay- wait behind the same birch tree. He was outsmarted by Betsy who was way out of his sight.

Darwin went home. He dropped his notepad on his never-made-up bed; his philosophy is why make it up when he has to sleep on it again and the civility of the surroundings and his room could be spoiled with the wind, with fire, with storms, and with earthquakes; but he mused the tsunami of man's behavior to his fellowman is worse than nature's disasters at times. Darwin thought the latest crimes in the United States are committed with guns remembering two days ago five people were killed in the Capital Gazette with guns, and Washington is doing nothing about the reckless use of guns.

He stopped thinking when the UPS man

rang his bell, and he handed him, Darwin, a letter. Darwin handed the UPS man five dollars and said thank you. He recognized the handwriting and opened the letter quickly. It was an invitation from his dear friend, Gloria Morancie. He reads: How are you, Darwin? Where are you vacationing—South Africa? If you are there, be back on time because I want you to be here for the co-naming of my husband's street on July 14, 2018, at noon. The street will be called by two names: Rockaway Parkway/ Horace L. Morancie Way. Darwin whispered, "I will only be calling the street Horace L. Morancie Way."

He had not heard from Gloria for quite a long time. He was happy to know Horace's full name would be seen as a bold landmark in Brooklyn because he was educated at Brooklyn Polytechnic University, Harvard University, Kennedy School of Government, Cornell University and Brooklyn Law School. He was the Director of Model Cities; he helped people in need; and he helped build decaying neighborhoods. Morancie's initiatives for the betterment of Brooklyn are in the fore of my memory. Whenever I praised him for what he had done for Brooklyn and its environs, he glided over my praises for him, and said, "I am just one of many."

But being in love with his wife, Gloria, was his fondest engagement.

Gloria and Horace were born in The Republic of Trinidad and Tobago (T&T). Gloria is a graduate of The College of New Rochelle and worked for the City as a social worker; and when Horace was alive she learned the art of politics from him. When Darwin visited Horace and Gloria at their lovely home on Rockaway Parkway, he always had a wonderful time. He had once told Horace, "Your educated wife doesn't only have book learning; she could cook, could sew, could clean, and could party nonstop. Did I leave out any of her qualifications, lover-boy Horace?"

Horace replied in deep Trini (T&T) accent. "Darwin boy, ah wish ah coulda tell you whaw you left out about me good-looking wife...."

Gloria, in equally rich Trini Ebonics, did not let her husband finish his sentence. "Horace, why you so fraid to tell Darwin whaw he leave out, and whaw we does do in de dark in the gallery for fun?"

Their laughter was riotous. And it was always so when the trio got together.

Darwin smiled, remembering all their jokes, then sat and had a sumptuous breakfast; but Dixie Dunkirk burned his thoughts when he remembered what she said about the female squirrel: "The woman's move is so romantic." He blamed himself for being so antisocial and should have replied to her statement; he thought to himself there are so many foolish men as he who cannot read the goodness in a woman's heart—her selflessness, her tenderness, her intuition, her kindness, her motherliness, and her caring. Still thinking, he thought of men who are still stuck in a time when a women's main function was only to procreate, and men rule their lives. Now women the world over are Presidents, Prime Ministers, Mayors, Doctors, Lawyers, Engineers, Scientists, Astronauts, the CEOs of Fortune 500 Companies, name it.

It was a beautiful morning at the end of spring and Darwin sat on his favorite, green bench in Baisley Pond Park. He went there for a reason: He loves to study people, immigrant people, and he loves to see some of them jogging in their panty-fitting shorts. He, too, is an immigrant in the United States for over fifty five years. He laughed on his way to the park when he denied giving Eldie a cell phone, and she shouted, "I hate you. Go back to your dumb country in Trinidad and Tobago and eat mangoes for your three meals." He shouted louder,

"I'm going to count the joggers—the educated and professional immigrants, especially those who own supermarkets—where you go to shop to buy sweet mangoes. Do you want to come and count those educated immigrants with me?"

"No! No! I have a bully in class; he's from your country; and I hope President Trump deports him."

Darwin had turned his back and pulled the sheet off of her. "Eldie, never let me hear you say President Trump should send back that boy! This country does not belong to President Trump or you. It belongs to all of us, and we came here last. Do you hear what I say, Eldie?"

"Yes, daddy."

"President Trump's first wife is an immigrant, and his present wife is also a newer immigrant. He has to deport of them before he and you deport the little boy in your class. See you later, Eldie. You know on which bench to find me today? Don't forget to make up your bed."

"Did you make my breakfast before you go to see your immigrant friends in the park?"

"Yes; I did. And don't forget your father who makes your breakfast is an immigrant, and he loves you; and he loves America too." He had hugged her, kissed her, and danced to the park.

The first sets of joggers were Asians wearing procedure masks; the next jogger was an old man who stopped jogging a yard away from Darwin. He stopped, smiled, and sat on the bench next to Darwin. A pair of joggers who chatted loudly, and another pair who looked as if their day is over walked by. Countless brisk walkers spoke many different languages, some said hello. Darwin introduced himself to the tired jogger who sat next to him. The man, a typical, suspicious New Yorker, just said, "Hi." He, purposely, did not tell Darwin his name. Darwin said, "Brother, I'm living less than fifty yards from this park, and I've been coming here over ten years. I love Queens. It has the most naturalized immigrant population in New York. Do you like Queens?"

The man shocked Darwin with his *non sequitur:* "Eight million Jehovah Witnesses don't salute the flag; two hundred thousand Amish don't stand for the National Anthem; one black man kneels, solemnly, and all hell breaks loose by that nondescript liar and racist in the White House. What do you think, Darwin?"

Darwin was so shocked by the question that he applied his daughter's strategy by asking him a question, too: "Did you tell me your name? I can't remember."

A group of Guyanese Indians drummed loudly, sang Indian songs, and danced. The women's beautiful mid-riffs moved sexually and Darwin's eyes feasted on their belly movements moving like shifting straws in the wind. He got off the bench, danced to the music, and said to the stranger sitting next to him, "Please, tell me your name, sir."

The man was again agitated. "God dammit it! Don't you know S stands for slave; I stands for I; R stands for remain? *Slave I Remain*. Darwin, I will never be a slave for you or any man."

Darwin stopped dancing, apologized for not knowing S.I.R means *Slave I Remain*, and he remained patiently to hear the man's name.

He stood up and looked Darwin in his eyes. "I am A'Ferti Ma'at Amun Re-El Native American of Aniyunwiya (Cherokee), Miccouskee, Creek, Seminole, Washita and Yamassee descent, and a white man."

"What!"

"Fool, don't you hear me? That's my name."

Darwin laughter was louder than the Guyanese tassa drums. "You? You... are a white man?

"Yes, fool. I am an indigenous man."

"Black-white man, why not shit in my mouth and call it butter."

"Your mouth is too ignorant for my knowledgeable shit. Your dig at me is an opinion. Let me be kind to you and quote my friend, Stacy Herbert, a businesswoman who lives in Tobago, West Indies: 'Everybody has an opinion as an anus.' I hope Herbert's simile didn't become laxatives."

Both laughed aloud.

Joggers had stopped, had listened to their conversations, and now Darwin found of a way of backing out of the discussion when A'Ferti pulled out from his cargo pants a document and started reading what the U.S. Census Bureau must adhere to when speaking about race and ethnicity. Darwin looked at his iPhone, and said, "Today is Saturday, and I have an important appointment in Brooklyn, A'Ferti."

He stretched his hand. “Can we meet another day to convince me why you are an indigenous white man? I will be on this very bench waiting for you.”

“Darwin, I will be here waiting to remind you when wisdom whispers, you should listen.”

“And I will be here to tell you if you have a dog, you don’t have to bark, A’Ferti.” Darwin released his hand from A’Ferti’s firm grip.

CHAPTER 2

It was July 14, 2018. The crowd of happy people, mainly people from the Caribbean, congregated at the northern intersection of Church Avenue and Rockaway Parkway were kissing Gloria Morancie as if she won the lotto and she was sharing the money won for their kisses. Two women jumbie mokos (women on stilts, fifteen feet tall), stood and guarded the new and covered street sign.

Speeches were made by countless friends praising the deceased, Horace L. Morancie, but Darwin hardly listened to any of the speeches until he heard the sultry voice of Carol-Ann Church, Gloria's daughter, on the dais reading: *Horace L. Morancie, today we honor your legacy. It is forever enshrined in the statutes of the City of New York that the north eastern corner of Rockaway Parkway and Church Avenue is co-named Horace L. Morancie Way. Your life's work will continue to influence New York movers and shakers for many more moons.*

Darwin questioned his thoughts, spoke to himself, and said, "I definitely know the person standing near Carol-Ann Church." A woman sitting next to him purposely stepped on his feet as he tried to move forward. Church was still speaking but Darwin was not hearing her because she was applauded loudly. He pushed himself through the vast crowd, got some hard elbows, but persevered until he was in the front row three yards away from the woman he thought he recognized. He looked at the woman as she walked carefully down the dais, and she spoke when she came next to him. "Darwin, I'm no longer a passenger on a golf cart in Baisley Pond Park. I'm now mobile by my body engine. Why are you looking at the street sign and not at me? Don't you recognize me, Mr. Antisocial?"

"Oh no! Oh no! I'm ashamed." He put his hand in the air.

"I hope, at least, you remember my name."

"Of course, Dixie Dunkirk. Are you a friend of Horace and Gloria Morancie?" He sang, "So nice to see you after Betsy outsmarted Tom."

Dixie applauded, kissed Darwin on both cheeks, and said, "Are you still antisocial?"

"I'm no longer in Baisley Pond Park where my moods swing daily, sometimes radically."

"Being in Baisley Pond Park, you thought I was Tom, and you were innocent Betsy?"

Darwin thought deeply. He opened his mouth to speak and closed it. He looked at Dixie from her head to her fashionable, heeled sandals, took in her truly-black-tender beauty for ten seconds, without saying a word, and wondered how come she looked so charming now. I want this Brooklyn beauty, he said in his mind.

Dixie said, "I'm waiting on an answer."

Gloria's voice is heard as thunder: "I'm going to count from one to ten. At ten, the covering on the sign will be removed." She counted to ten.

The two women jumbie mokos towering in the air like high-flying kites removed the cloth covering and the bold, new co-name of the street, HORACE L. MORANCIE WAY, is seen. The mammoth crowd increased with Trinis, screamed, "Horace L. Morancie Way!"

But Gloria Morancie heralded, "My husband! My husband! Horace L. Morancie Way will be seen from our porch! May God bless my deceased husband. I had loved him with all my heart."

The crowd shouted incessantly Horace L. Morancie Way, people hugged each other, some in tears, said, "Horace was the best; he helped us all; St. Peter is waiting on him to help with his prioritized community engagements in heaven."

Dixie hugged Darwin, loosely. Darwin pulled her in, firmly, kissed her lips, and she parted them for penetration. He accepted the space, and their love story began. Each told the other titbits of their lives, present, and past.

"Darwin, I was eight years old. Florence, my mother, held my hand firmly as we traversed the streets of Brooklyn, sleeping couple nights in Marine Park. We looked into each house on every street on a steaming day. On New York Avenue girls were skipping, jumping in and out of ropes, forward and backwards. I was walking backwards and looking at them and felt the tug-forward movement of my mother's coarse left hand. Something was wrong with her right hand. I knew what was wrong with her right hand but she never told me when I asked."

"Dixie, parents never speak of their pains or their sacrifices to their children; they swallow their griefs and sadness."

"You don't have to tell me that! When I could no longer look at the children skipping, I began looking at white people's houses and their manicured lawns. We were now on Bedford Avenue, and I wondered why my mother was going south. My palm was sweaty; she would not let it go; and I had asked, 'Ma, where are you taking me?'"

"Where God leads me, child."

"What are you looking for, Ma?" I knew, but I wanted her to say it, so I forced it out of her.

"A place for us to live, Dixie."

"Why did you leave where we were living?" Now we were way down Avenue U and Batchelder Street, about seven miles or more away from our beginning point.

"It is a long story, and children should not be told parents' sad and long stories because those long stories addle their brains, Dixie."

Dixie chose to call her mother Florence

to feel, she, Dixie, is sensible as an adult and could be told long and sad stories. "Florence, I am eight, and I am smart as if I am eighty, so tell me any long story that you are not happy about. I know why you are looking for a place to live."

Florence was shocked to see a black child, five years old, riding his bicycle in the neighborhood inhabited completely by white people. She was tired looking into houses, knocking doors, and asking white landlords, "I am looking for an apartment or a room for me and my daughter. Do you have any to rent?" The answer was always, "Sorry," or "We just rented the last apartment."

The little boy pulled up his bicycle next to Dixie, and she said the words to the little boy that her mother had been saying for the past four hours to white adults but in a friendly way. "Hi, my name is Dixie. What's yours?"

"Jason."

"Jason, I see you live in a nice house."

"And it is big."

"Your mother has a room to rent for me and my mother. We are homeless. Last night we slept in Marine Park."

"Ask Aunt Ruby. She helps everybody. Dixie, you can sleep in my room because it is too big for me alone to sleep in...."

Dixie came back to the present moment, squeezed Darwin's hand as if to bring him to focus on what she was saying, and she said, "Darwin, it was the first time Florence in more than four hours released my palm from her grip and clasped her both palms to pray. I asked Florence, 'Is it here God leads you?' Before she answered me, Jason shouted again, 'Ask Aunt Ruby. She helps everybody.'"

A hand touched Darwin and Dixie's shoulders simultaneously. "You two know each other?" Gloria Morancie asked, still bubbling with joy from seeing the mammoth crowd of families, friends, and strangers at her husband's ceremony.

"Sure," Dixie answered.

"How come I don't know that? You and I were at college together; I know Darwin because he was an acolyte of Horace; and he is always in our house. Are you, Dixie Dunkirk and Darwin Wolmers, two hills that became lovers and hid your love life from me?" Gloria surveyed their eyes.

Darwin answered, but exaggerated. "We met some years ago in Baisley Pond Park."

"In daylight or on a bench when the park was pitch dark?" Gloria smiled cunningly.

"It was daylight when a tomcat was trying to catch a female squirrel for lunch," Dixie said.

"Did Miss Squirrel get eaten by the Mr. Tom?"

Darwin quickly answered. "Miss Squirrel is a woman, and when wisdom whispered in her brain, she branched from tree to tree like cheetah going to find Tarzan to tell him Jane is in trouble, and Mr. Tom hadn't the IQ to catch Miss Squirrel for his lunch."

"To you, humans, who caught whom in Baisley Pond Park?" Gloria laughed vulgarly, and said, "Horace would have answered my question politically and tell you how we met; but he's dead. Let me leave you two lovebirds alone." She thanked Dixie for coming and for telling people of Horace's varied, prioritized community engagements. She walked up to Darwin and whispered in his ear, "All the college boys and men in New Rochelle had tried to get her in bed, without success. Good luck, liar." She kissed his cheeks, pinched him, and walked away.

Dixie stopped telling Darwin her life story. Nevertheless, Darwin was eager to know what happened when Jason jumped off his bike and called his Aunt Ruby. But with the tears dripping from Dixie's eyes, he ended his curiosity.

"Dixie, here's my number; you don't have to give me yours."

"Why?"

"I was just pretending."

"Was that a pretend kiss you gave me when you pulled me into you as a rapist?"

"No. I wanted to do that in Baisley Pond Park too." They laughed. "Can I call Uber for you?"

"Are you now trying to get my address on your phone?"

They laughed aloud.

Uber came on his call, and he opened the door for her.

She said, “Hope to see you soon to get another pretend kiss, and to hear your story too, Darwood.”

“Why you change win to wood?”

“Win is non-erectile, so I prefer Wood, the other guy, instead.”

Even when Darwin opened his door he was still laughing at what Dixie last said.

Eldika shouted: “You were not here to greet me when I came home from school.”

“Eldie, forgive me. I went to see the opening of the Horace L. Morancie Way. You know Mr. Morancie and I were buddies.”

“I called Mrs. Morancie, and she told me the ceremony was over long ago. Why did you come home so late? This morning I told you I was not feeling well, and you forced me to go to school.”

“I told Miss Jenkins who babysits you when I’m not at home to use my car, pick you up, bring you home, and stay with you till I come. Did she bring you home?”

"Yes. I don't like her, and I told her to leave because I don't need a babysitter."

"She should not have listened to you and leave. What else you told her?"

"To stop trying to be my mother, and she is ugly."

The phone rang, and Eldika answered, "Hello."

"May I speak to Darwood?"

"Whoever you are, there's no Darwood living here. The name is Darwin."

"I'm very sorry. May I speak to Darwin."

"Please, don't make that mistake again. Who are you?"

"My name is Dixie Dunkirk. And what's your name?"

"My name is Eldika Wolmers, but my father calls me Eldie."

"So you are Darwin's daughter?"

"Yes, I am."

"May I, please, speak to your father, Eldika?"

"Hold on." She called her father and handed him the phone.

"Hello," Darwin said.

"Your daughter censured me for changing the suffix win to wood."

"You are lucky we no longer have phones we can slam down."

"I hope she will welcome me when you invite me to your home. Tell me not what she needs, but what she wants and I'll get it for her."

"Are you trying to bribe my daughter to have me for yourself?"

"I'll do anything to get you in or out of Baisley Pond Park to be my best friend." She hung up. She was afraid of getting a negative answer. She called five minutes after she hung up and said, "What Eldika wants?"

"A laptop. Is that too much for you?"

"Are you investigating the worth of my pocket? I'm richer than Donald Trump. His airlines failed; his casinos failed; his marriages failed; his mortgages failed; his fake university failed; his vodka failed; he had six bankruptcies. You want to hear more of Trump's business failures?"

"Not at all. Eldie and I will invite you for dinner next week."

"How should I dress? I suspect from our short questions-and-answers chat that she's precocious, direct, and bossy. I hope with the laptop, she'll like me without being dressed in Givenchy Haute Couture."

"I see you are going all out to bribe my Princess, but she'll prefer you to be a jeans-and-T-shirt girl. I change my mind because with that look I may want to touch the nipples pointing north in your T-shirt, so let it be business on top and athletic at the bottom; that's a modern look from Halston."

"I'll do anything to get closer to you." Again she hung up, not wanting to hear an equivocating answer from Darwin. Somehow, she thought, he was different from the other men she dated. She had listened to those men's every word, parsed their sentences as they spoke, and gave them her answer not waiting to hear more of their slick lines that they practiced and used on gullible women.

Dixie, at nineteen, thinking her mother and Aunt Ruby's advice was old-fashioned, left home, shacked up with another girl much older than she, fell in love with a senior guy when in college, and the hurt was painful when he walked out of her life after abusing her sexually. She vowed, with tears dripping, never to be a "too nice" woman and came to the conclusion men love breaking nice women's hearts. She was in the company of other girls going home crying after college day was over. Those inexperienced girls, as she ignorant about adult life and heartbreaks, were in need of a man for the wrong reasons. Now men—no men—will make her take off her Victoria's secrets, especially if they didn't buy them. And those she bought were skimpy and expensive. Not that she'll be an office bitch, whom other women would hate when she's employed, or a strap-hanger bitch who rushes the old man for the only empty seat in the crowded subway saying to him, "Didn't your mama sixty years ago teach you to give women your seat?"

She remembered going to bed nightly, crying, couldn't overcome another hurt, finals were coming, and she couldn't concentrate on her studies because Harvey, the classmate she loved, loved another girl. But as she traced her past misfortune in love, Darwin seemed different from other men cheaters; and she'll win him by loving his daughter, and he'll love her. Her mind was forever traveling backward to a sociology class when the professor called on students to express any of two basic feelings—love or hate. Those who labored their feelings on love got the bigger audience. But the student from North Korea said, "I will grieve if I didn't hate the dictator who caused me to leave my home after he murdered my brother."

The teacher asked, "Who'd second the motion of hate?"

Dixie stood up. "I'd hate the man, as much as Chulen hates the dictator who killed her brother, who takes off my Victoria's secrets without my consent, then goes to a woman who buys her drawers from a dollar store."

She came back to the present moment when she told Darwin the class study, and he couldn't end his laughter.

"If you do that to me, Darwin, I'd hate you with the combination of my and Chulen's hatred."

"The fact is those other men were not really in love with you; I am. So you will be the one who'd be pulling off your Victoria's secrets, and I may not want them pulled."

"I won't compromise myself."

"My wife told me the same thing but made a child for another man. She was swept over by another man for his romantic fantasy because mine had become stale. Her friends who advised her to choose the newer romantic fantasy were blind, and although she had one eye, she listened to them. My wife didn't graduate. You did. Now you are working for enough money to buy Eldie a laptop, not from a bargain store, but from Amazon."

"You can buy Alexa Echo from Amazon for me to hear Nancy Wilson singing *Guess Who I Saw Today*? She asked her lover that question as they sat at the dinner table."

Darwin answered, and smiled: "Nancy Wilson told her lover, 'I saw you with your lover when I thought I was your lover.' Dixie, my dear, I hope you don't have goat mouth and predict coming events."

"All I have is the presence of mind always, and how to pull the plug before the avalanche of more misfortune in love covers me."

"Which means you are not the 'too-nice' type of women? My only advice is: Do not spell out all your dislikes immediately in the future for me to hear."

"I started telling you what happened to me and my mother when we saw Jason on his bicycle."

"And you stopped."

"I'm glad I did."

"Why?"

"I should have told you then friendship lasts longer than love."

"When we play by our own rules."

"Sometimes we need an umpire."
"Never for your own rule?"

"Yes, sometimes. What do you think?"

Darwin always equivocated with his answers because of his wife's betrayal. But he was in love, silently, with Dixie. In their lovemaking he refrained from saying, I love you. He would say, you are a beautiful woman; you dress better than all the women I dated. When she had asked, do I dress better than your wife? he had said, leave her out when we are in bed. Sometimes she wanted to spice up the mood but was afraid to talk about her likes when in bed, a part of lovemaking she relished early in womanhood when she dated older men.

She had told him, "Before we have sex, let's see the same doctor and you can choose the doctor."

He had replied, "Do you think I'll give you a disease?"

She answered, "Since you don't trust women, why trust me? I can give STD's to you."

Their nightly conversations sometimes turned into wars. Once he had asked her, "When last you got laid?"

She answered nastily. "The same time your wife got fucked and got pregnant for Harvey."

Shocked, he asked, "You know Harvey?"

"He left me for your wife. All of us attended College New Rochelle."

Neither of them called each other in a month. One night her phone rang without salutation from the caller. "Okay, let's go to your doctor."

She replied, "Let's go to Donald Trump's

doctor. He gives perfect diagnoses, without seeing his patient."

Darwin's laughter was thunderous. Eldika rushed in her father's room and asked why he laughed so loudly. "Miss Dixie, the woman we invited for dinner, who gave you the laptop, gave me a nice joke."

"I like Miss Dixie very much. When next she comes for dinner I will tell her what Wendy's mother always says about Prince Harry's birth and why he married a brown woman. Can I tell you first?"

"I told you before don't tell me what you heard from the Lady Pope on TV, and never tell Miss Dixie or anybody for that matter."

"Why?"

"You are older now and since you were a little girl I had told you never repeat gossips, not even those gossips from the Lady-Pope gossiper of pop culture on the TV. She doesn't tell people about her life, which, I am sure hers is in a bad mess."

Eldika had been telling her father that she wants Miss Dixie to come and live with them. Coming home one day she saw Miss

Dixie in the kitchen preparing dinner. She shouted, "Miss Dixie, Miss Dixie! You come at last." She ran to Dixie and their embrace took minutes. "Miss Dixie, why don't you and daddy get married?"

"Eldika, there is a word in courtship before marriage called proposal."

"When daddy and I speak of how people in a family should love each other, he never speaks of a proposal."

"Your daddy equivocates. You know what that means?"

"Sure! He is always like that. When I ask him what are we having for dinner, do you know what his answer usually is?"

"No."

"Guess."

Darwin was listening to their conversation, and he walked in softly. "You two women are gossiping about me and using that big word equivocating while the bank had me working late, correcting items in difficulty, and speaking to the traders. I have not had an increase in two years. I think I will retire from that part-time job again."

"Daddy, today I had to explain in class what equivocating means."

"Tell me, Princess Eldie."

"I want you to stop equivocating when you speak to Miss Dixie. If she asks you if you love her, give her a direct answer. Stop beating about the bush. That's equivocating. My mother told me that's why you and she always quarreled."

He walked to the bedroom.

Dixie's ginger ale dropped from her hand to the floor. She rushed to mop it up. Eldika stopped her. "Let dad do that when he comes from the bedroom. The #MeToo Movement began in this house with my mother, but a male judge gave full custody of me to dad."

"Did your daddy tell you why the judge did that?"

"No."

Darwin came from the bedroom, mopped the wet floor, then said, "Don't let summer leave us. Let's pack a night basket and head to Coney Island."

"Miss Dixie, daddy doesn't wear shorts, bathing trunks, or anything above his knees. When I visited Mammy she told me he told her from the day he came out of short pants, he never put on one again. He has nice legs, but I don't know why he hides them."

"You ever saw his legs?"

"Of course! We live at the same address."

Dixie laughed and laughed and laughed. She likes Eldika's cheerfulness towards her; she felt Eldika approved of her father's relationship with her, and wouldn't be surprised if Eldika tells her father to marry her. In their drive to Coney Island, Eldika said, "Miss Dixie, would you like to be my stepmother? I'm warning you, as I warned other women who visited us, you can be possessive of him, but not in my presence."

"If we are married, and I pass my hand in his hair in your presence, would you be annoyed?"

"Those nails you have are like claws. You can hurt my father."

Darwin spoke to his daughter when their eyes met in the car mirror, and she saw his frown.

"Miss Dixie, I'm sorry."

He said, "Eldie and Dixie, I'm going to shock both of you today."

"Daddy, are you going to wear a short bathing trunk today?"

"That's right, Miss Peace Maker."

"Miss Dixie, you being here makes me happy. I want to see plenty signs of your lipstick on my daddy's pillows and sheets when I come from upstate next month."

"Can I call you Eldie?"

"Of course, Miss Dixie."

"I thank you, Eldie, for your present and future permission. Is your laptop still working?"

"Was that a bribe?"

"Of course not, Eldie. Bribes only last from sunrise on Monday till sunset on Tuesday. Our friendship would be permanent."

Somehow Darwin didn't want those two females to be together for long. He was afraid his daughter would speak of her mother's infidelity to Dixie which she heard from people. He, too, had his brand of infidelity in the marriage to his wife, and his daughter knew of his infidelity, too, from her mother, but pretended she did not know.

CHAPTER 3

Eldika graduated from middle school, and she was in high school. Dixie stopped questioning herself of what is the right decision, and, finally, moved in to live fully with Darwin and Eldika in Queens, New York. She loved to sit in the sun in Baisley Pond Park, and whenever Darwin told her to get out of the sun because she's sufficiently black, she told him that she wants to get blacker because her white boyfriend (she invented one at that time) likes her blackness and he, Darwin, may have to compete with her white boyfriend. Her laughter could be heard by other sunbathers in the park. Darwin was not amused, and she loved making him get jealous. Because of his strict behavior and his jealousy, she was not ready to take the plunge into matrimony.

One morning Eldika said, "Miss Dixie, daddy told me he proposed to you in earnest—I learned that new word today — and you said he should wait a little more. When is a little more—one year, two years, how many years?"

"Eldie, we are married in love, and we have deep feelings for each other; our deep affection for each other is just not recorded in the Registrar at City Hall. We have joint checking and saving accounts; and, most important, we are making plans for you to go to college."

"I hope not the way my mother and father had planned about you."

"What do you mean?"

"You are a big woman. You know what the hell I mean, Miss Dixie."

Darwin jumped in the conversation. "Eldie, what language is that?"

"The language I heard you and my mother spoke, day in and day out. People tell me about the way you and my mother behaved." She walked away and slammed her bedroom door.

Dixie and Darwin looked at each other. Dixie knew Darwin avoided confrontation, but she meant to back him into a corner where he had no choice but to fight his way out of that corner and answer her. She understood what Eldie said, and she addressed it.

“Darwin, I have already told you your wife took my man from me in college.” She looked at him. “Don’t stop me from talking and walk away as your daughter and slam your bedroom door on me.

"This is your house, not mine. In your proposal to me, I could see that was an empty proposal. You were proposing to give Eldie her wish; it was not (she emphasized) your genuine wish. In the beginning your time in bed with me was heavenly. Now I can see your disgust, your boredom, and you shower immediately after sex as if my body is mud. Before, you wrapped me in your arms, and we showered next morning, doing it again in the tub. You expect me to believe your love is fresh as when we met at Horace L. Morancie Way. Then, in broad daylight, you pulled my tongue to find my tonsils; you pinched my arse, over and over; you played with my nipples while you drove; and you laid me couple times on park benches and said the park was a good place to have me looking at the moonlit sky. Now you purposely delay to come in bed. There’s no more cunnilingus.” She looked at him. “Thanks, for not interrupting me.” She pulled her chair back.

He pulled his chair forward. "Sit down, please. It's my turn to speak. Your man, Harvey, was my friend. I told him about you when I saw you in the park, and by describing you he knew exactly who you are. I didn't know who you are, and I didn't wish to know. In describing you, he said you are a trickster; you walk with men on your forehead; and you rule by the neck. Is that true?"

"I stopped my trickery since I met you, Mr. Wolmers."

"How am I to know?"

"Whom do you believe—the nominee Brett Kavanaugh whom it is alleged two women said he exposed his private part to them or Christine Blasey Ford, the woman, it is alleged, he raped when she was a teenager?"

"I can't give an answer because I do not listen to that kind of politics on TV about big-shot white people when so many poor, black, white, and brown children go to bed hungry each night."

"You called a woman's name in our sex act last night. Who's she? Could you give an answer to that?"

He wouldn't answer.

Eldie rushed from her bedroom, hugged Dixie, and said, "Miss Dixie, I'm sorry for the way I spoke to you. Please, forgive me. I apologize."

"Let me kiss you, my little darling. Do you think my kiss is a bribe too?"

"Oh no, Miss Dixie!"

They all laughed.

"Darwin, my love, you can go for your morning walk in the park and watch those thick women with big bottoms in undersized shorts go by. Eldie and I have to make up for all those days she was away. Now that she is graduating from high school and going to York College and will be coming home every day, we'd be two peas in a pod."

Darwin said, softly, "Dixie, you will never complain of my masculinity in bed if I could call my ex-wife's name and tell you what that woman did to make me come to bed early." He laughed aloud.

"Honey, what sweetens you?"

"Just the thought of you knowing Valentine's Day is coming, and I will buy you thirteen long-stem roses without thorns."

"Why thirteen and not twelve?"

"I heard Harvey gave you twelve, and I want to top him."

"What else you heard and rehearsed to fuck me so sweetly?" She wore a broad smile.

"You and his other woman had a fight." His dimple deepened.

"What's the other woman's name?" She laughed vulgarly.

"You know her name too! Why not call it. You are afraid to?"

"Eldie is not here, so tell me what she does to put energy in your groins, and I'll do it even better tonight. Darwood, tell me, please." She lowers her voice and sits on his lap. "I checked all the rooms. Eldie is not here. Tell me what your wife did, and I'll do it." She pulled his penis.

"I don't want to do it. My mind is on business."

"I am younger than you; you are middle

aged; and Eldie's upbringing should be our only business. Somehow, you think I'm winning Eldie's love, which you didn't want to happen. You don't like confrontation because you don't want to hear the truth. You have to go with me in bed. Now! And I will tell you what I like, and how Harvey did it. I will even do what Geena did because Harvey told me what she did when they went to a motel. And what she did, and he had liked it; I will do that too to see if you will like it."

She did not have to pull Darwin to the bed. He pulled her. He was satisfied with her new performance. He jumped off the bed, pulled a little box out of his pants pocket, opened it, and said, "Isn't it your size?"

She screamed. "Who told you?"

"Forget who told me. Would you let me put it on?"

"Yes! Yes!"

He knelt. "Dixie, this is your engagement ring. Would you marry me?"

"One hundred yes even though it could have been in a better surrounding with a swallow flying around."

"But one swallow doesn't make a summer."

"For me, one swallow would be fine because it will bring good news from my lover."

He put the ring on her finger, kissed her deep, and said, "The indigenous man will be my witness."

"Eldie will be mine. Only two witnesses we need."

He looked through the window, saw Eldie with someone in the distance, and said, "Honey, Darwood has to go to the post office before it is closed to mail a package to his sister, Cintie, in London." He drove off.

Eldika's footstep dragged, and she called out, "Miss Dixie, I want you to meet my friend, Bobby."

Dixie quickly put on her robe and washed her hands thoroughly. "How are you, Bobby?" She stretched her hand. "I am Dixie."

"I am fine, Miss Dixie. Eldika always talks about you. She told me you are a nice lady, and you will not protest my friendship with her because I am white."

"Of course not! You are very handsome."

He smiled. "She told me she doesn't know what her father will say."

"Her father is not here, but he'll be back soon. You and Eldie can play video games, and I will get something for both of you to snack on."

"I am not hungry, Miss Dixie," Bobby said.

"Please, bring something for both of us, Miss Dixie. He'll enjoy the cake you baked last night. I'll make the lemonade with brown sugar. To me, brown sugar gives a better flavor to everything than that white sugar as Bobby."

"Eldika, I hope that is a joke?"

"Of course, it is a joke, Bobby. Don't be so thin-skinned."

Dixie, Eldika, and Bobby were snacking and chitchatting when Darwin came home. Bobby stood and introduced himself. "I am Bobby, Eldika's BFF."

"Bobby, I am Darwin. It's the first time I heard my daughter's last name is BFF."

"BFF means best friends forever, Mr. Darwin. I am white; my BFF is brown. I hope you don't mind."

"Brown?" Darwin opened his eyes wide. "I thought my daughter is black."

Dixie spoke with her eyes. "Darwin, please, do not interrupt him. Let him speak. Go-ahead, Bobby."

"Mr. Darwin, do you hate me because I am white?"

"Why do you ask me that question, Bobby?"

"Eldika was somewhat afraid to let me meet you?"

"Was she afraid to let you see and meet Miss Dixie, Bobby?"

"Not at all. She said she and Miss Dixie are close."

"You listen to politics on the TV a lot, Bobby?"

"No; I only read of politics on my cell, and on social media platforms. But in my house my mother listens to that politics stuff day and night. She likes President Trump; he is her hero; and whenever she bites bread, she calls his name."

"Why?"

"I never asked her."

"In your house people talk race politics?"

"Yes. My sister, Erin, left home, and she she's living with her black boyfriend because of what my mother told her in anger. Erin and mother quarreled, and Erin told mother she should never mix her words with her mood because she'll have many options to change her mood, but she may never get an opportunity to replace her spoken word."

"What did your mother say when Erin left?"

"Nice things and ugly things, according to how she got up on mornings."

"Do you want to tell me some of the nice things or ugly things?"

"No."

"I'm sorry to ask."

"You couldn't know my answer if you didn't ask."

Dixie changed their conversation. "Who needs to taste my delicious, carrot cake?"

Darwin meant to keep the discussion flowing. "Who thinks the #MeToo advocate's carrot cake should not control politics?"

"Me!" Eldie said.

"Me!" Bobby said.

"Me! The ayes have it," Dixie said the loudest.

The morning conversation ended when Bobby said, "Mr. Darwin, can I visit your home again and continue our friendly conversation?"

"Only if I'm your second BFF."

Dixie shouted, "I'm his second BFF. You are third, Darwood."

"Miss Dixie and Mister," he paused hearing the name Darwood for the first time.

"That was a mistake, Bobby. He's Mr. Darwin."

"Miss Dixie and Mr. Darwin, I love both suffixes to Dar."

"Me, too," Eldika shouted. And everyone laughed.

Bobby stopped laughing and said, "I'll tell my mother to invite both of you for dinner on my birthday. Would you mind if I recite my favorite poem for you, Mr. Darwin, that I will recite on my birthday to know why people shouldn't lose the common touch?"

"Recite it. I love poems. I will let you read mine one day when you visit us again."

Bobby recited Rudyard Kipling's poem, If, solemnly, and his diction was perfect. Tears welled in Darwin's eyes as Bobby repeated the lines:

If you can talk with crowds and keep your virtue,

Or walk with kings—nor lose the common touch.

He looked Darwin in his eyes, bowed, and said, "Mr. Darwin, if I have all those qualities, would you object to my being your daughter's best friend forever? And if forever realizes, would you be happy if that realization is with a white man?"

"Which white man?"

"With me, when I'm a man, Mr. Darwin?"

"Yes." He hugged Bobby.

A week later, Darwin took an envelope from the mailbox. The envelope was embossed in thick, white paper. He handed the envelope to Dixie. "This is yours."

She looked at the envelope. "Darwood, the first addressee is your name."

"Darwood?" He smiled. "Okay, it's Darwin I see. I'll open it." He silently read the words written on the embossed card enclosed, and he handed the card to Dixie. She read aloud: Mr. and Mrs. Oliver Bradford invite Darwin Wolmers, Eldika Wolmers, and Dixie Waltz Dunkirk to their son, Bobby's Eighteenth Birthday Party. R.S.V.P.

"How the hell she knows my full name?" Dixie said.

"She's probably the woman the little boy on the bicycle called out to help you when you and your mother were homeless and looking for a place to rest your bodies. By the way, you never finished telling me about that very sad time in your life."

"Many times I attempted to tell you, and you always cut me off. You want me to tell it today?"

"Sure! Provided you want to pull me back on the bed and give me some of the goodies you gave Harvey."

"You damaged my pearl last night by calling Harvey's name over and over in jealousy."

"I read a little jealousy in a relationship is healthy; and it is nice to know I am afraid to lose you."

"Harvey spoke French and Portuguese to enter, and Japanese and Spanish to exit."

"I never knew you had an international pearl between your legs. Had Donald Trump known about your pearl, he would have refused Stormy Daniel's."

They laughed so much that they could not continue their sex act.

"Miss Dunkirk, I think you accepted my proposal and took that engagement ring because Harvey's international dick is like the dough man's—soft."

"But he bred your wife."

"You ever heard of the proverb: Every cloud has a silver lining?"

"Who's that silver lining?"

"You! You! You, babe."

"Don't call me babe."

"Don't be so sensitive, babe."

"I've told you before: Never call me babe."

"Why?"

"From babe you'll be calling me bitch."

"I will never call you by that B-word."

"Let's get back to the invitation from the Bradfords." She called Eldika at the college basketball game. "We got an invitation from Bobby's parents to come to Bobby's birthday party. We'd see his mother and father?"

"Bobby's father doesn't live there, Miss Dixie. He only visits."

"Where he lives?"

"Bobby doesn't know, but he told me his mother is rich, and she invests in the stock market."

"She's going to have a big bash?"

"Bobby told me she always had big parties."

"Your name is on the invitation, Eldie."

"I know."

"Is Bobby your boyfriend?"

"Miss Dixie, he's a friend, and he's male."

"That evasive answer is telling me that's not my business."

"No, Miss Dixie. If I say yes, you'll tell dad who, from since I was little, told me to keep away from white men."

"Why?"

"Because ... I don't want to say it now; probably another time."

"If he disagrees, I'll let him know you're old enough to choose your friends. How old are you now?"

"Nineteen."

When Eldika got home, Dixie looked at Eldika in a motherly way. "Come closer to me, little girl. When did you get those curvy hips? I am jealous of them. Do boys whistle when you walk by?"

She blushed and smiled.

"Blacks, whites, Hispanics, half breeds—which group?"

"I visited my mother last week, and she asked me those same questions. I was three months old when the judge gave me, officially, to my father."

"Eldie, I was eight years old when my mother and I were homeless."

"You, you, were homeless?"

"Yes, I was."

"Who got a place for you to live?"

"A five-year-old boy named Jason."

"True?"

"True, true. He called his Aunt Ruby and told her that he alone lives in his big room, and he's frightened, and he'd like me to sleep in the room with him."

"And where did your mother sleep?"

"Eldie, her accommodation was satisfying. I want to write about our homelessness after your father and I get married." She paused. "If we ever get married."

"Why the subjunctive *If*, Miss Dixie?"

"Sometimes I use If, the subjunctive, loosely."

"I would like to hear the end of your sad story before you write about it."

"I will tell you from the beginning to the end of my present life if you conduct yourself as a lady when you are among boys—black, white, brown, yellow, all colors."

"Bobby included?"

"Isn't he male?"

"He's twenty one."

"Twenty-one-year-olds too can become fathers." Eldie was now in the porch when Dixie spoke to her.

Darwin came and interrupted them. "Ladies, how should I behave at the birthday party?"

"Dad, Bobby said his mother is a Donald-Trump's addict, and she has not forgiven Barack Obama when he said white people hold on to their bible and their guns. Stay away from politics. Bobby told me she invites people at her dinners with the aim of discussing politics and to advise people to vote for President Trump for him to have a second term because he is responsible for the stock market rising every day."

"Before the millennials start dancing their shoes off, could I ask Bobby to recite If for me?"

"Dad, he'd love to. His aim is to be in movies."

"And you will be his co-star?" Dixie asked.

Darwin raised his voice. "Not my daughter!"

"Dad, 'co' means equal."

"I too think 'co' means equal." Dixie confirmed.

"I can settle the score by not going to that white boy's party."

"Dad, he's not a boy."

"Because you are in college, you are correcting my English, too."

"Darwin, your daughter is not correcting your English, she is correcting your racist thinking."

"Now you are my Baisley Pond Park sociologist teacher?"

"No, I'm not so smart. I am the woman in this long, roundabout courtship who is thinking whether marrying you is my lacking common sense. By seeing how you continue to be unreasonable in your behavior towards your daughter, you will be same to me, or worse."

"You are now the female Dr. Phil."

"For sure, I will never be that nice babe you'll soon be calling bitch on overdrive. Today, sarcastically, you call me Baisley Pond Park sociologist by way of your Appreciation Deficit Disorder. No wonder why you want to know what happened when I was eight years old and homeless to trace me out. If you are still in your potty-training days, I'm not. I've been noticing you."

"My black beauty, what have you noticed?"

"You have taken me for granted; I'm now your house ho."

"Whore?"

"Yes. You hop on me whenever you want sex without foreplay or romance. You have stopped bringing me flowers since the week after the Horace L. Morancie Way ceremony in Brooklyn. You dress up like a Christmas tree with clean and sexy underpants to go for long drives without me and return late, unlike when we first met. Since your sister, Cintie, left two years ago to return to London, you don't even invite me to go in the park with you to watch the blooming lilies, to hug, to talk, to laugh joyously, and to watch the joggers go by speaking so many different languages and saying hello to me."

"But I'm here with you. I don't sleep out."

"You are so silent most nights with your face facing the wall that I wished you slept out and go looking for your beloved wife, that you are still grieving for her romance. Lucky Harvey!"

"How many times I have to tell you that woman and I have been divorced since Eldika was three months old."

"But you still call her name when we are in bed. She was locked down waiting on your ring. The engagement ring you gave me is squeezing my fuckin finger. Why not pawn it and give your wife the money? I feel like running away now in this slipper and dirty apron I'm wearing and cooking for you."

"The way you underrate me, you should. You are not a beginner in love affairs so you can run and pick up an educated man of your college choice tonight. For that matter, you are accustomed running out on men."

"Just as your hot, over-trained wife ran out on you. When my time comes to run, who knows, I may give you at least a week's notice."

"Miss Dixie and dad, please, stop. My

head is bursting open. I want to scream," Eldika said.

Dixie rushed into the bedroom, slammed the door, and shouted, "You're a fuckin bully."

Darwin whistled, as Frank Sinatra sang the words of the tune, "Insensitive," What Can I Do When a Love Affair is Over?

"Dad, the love affair is not over. Both of you are too highly strung this morning. Too much sugar in your love. Dad, this argument started because Miss Dixie objected to the way you were defining me in a limited way, as a fool."

"Because I have my suspicion of that white boy."

"I think you hate white people."

"They hate us too."

She tapped his knees. "Do they hurt?"

"Just a little."

"Then I think it's time to go and wait on the green bench in the park for your new friend, A'Ferti, the Cherokee. He will give you some Indian remedy."

“That woman slammed the door on me, but I know she’s waiting anxiously on the day when I will name the date of our marriage.”

“That’s a bully’s boast, dad. To me, she’s not in a hurry. That day may never come.” She tells her father to come closer to her.

He came.

“Daddy, say after me: Behold, God is my helper; the Lord sustains my life.”

He repeated those words after her. “Who taught you to say Psalm 54:6?”

“Whenever I visit my mother, and I am leaving, she and I say that psalm. It is now my MO, my *modus operandi.*”

“You are using big words on me.”

“True words for both of us to think and not be judgmental, dad.”

CHAPTER 4

Darwin made three rounds in the park to prove to himself, not to his daughter, that the pain in his knees is minor. Winded, he sat on his favorite green bench hoping his new friend, A'Ferti Ma'at, who calls himself the original indigenous man, and who says he's white, according to how he interpreted the U.S. Office of Personnel Management Guide to Personnel Data Standards. Darwin practiced pronouncing A'Ferti's full name correctly, and he knew A'Ferti would be impressed with his pronunciation. He also researched what A'Ferti told him about who is a white man, different from what is cast around loosely by people. Darwin was lost in his research of what fact is and what fiction is, and he ended his research.

Like a child first learning the letters of the alphabet, and getting more confused as he tries to be of the same understanding as A'Ferti who says he is white, Darwin read aloud the information in his hand not noticing A'Ferti was on the green bench:

Form 181: White: A person having origins in any of the original people of Europe, the Middle East, or North Africa....

A voice is heard adding words to what is not in Form 181..."where they just discovered the remains of the oldest bones in Europe were that of a Melaninite white male...I am of that blood as black as I am." A'Ferti touched Darwin. "Have you anything to say to that, my brother?"

"I believe you, and all your knowledge of such things." That was Darwin's way of getting away from a long discussion that A'Ferti would have introduced for the rest of the afternoon in trying to indoctrinate Darwin in his, A'Ferti's, belief.

"So you see my logic?"

Darwin nodded. "A'Ferti, I waited here to tell you I want you to be a witness in my marriage."

"To a Melaninite woman as I?"

"She's a beautiful woman. That's all I know of her background."

"Tell me the date, and I shall be there."

"I'll apprise you, but, please, no gift when that date comes."

"My only gift to your wife and you will be these words: THINK! WHEN WISDOM WHISPERS."

"I have been telling my wife-to-be if she has a dog, she doesn't have to bark."

"Those are unkind words, unless you are the dog. Take it from this Cherokee, she jots down all your unkind sayings, and she will remind you of them at the opportune time."

They parted company.

Darwin made another lap of the circle. As usual, the circle was filled with joggers, fast and slow walkers, caregivers holding their clients carefully as they slowly walked by, and Asian women, as was expected, wore procedure masks that covered their mouths and noses. Darwin laughed and introduced himself to the one-legged man with the sign on his back: AM FLORIDIAN. WHERE CAN I FIND GOOD

HOOKAS? Darwin laughed louder when the one-legged man told him why he wants good hookahs. That morning more foreign languages were heard, and placards, political and funny, were in the hands of Caribbean people who sang calypsos and danced while exercising. Darwin danced a bit to Calypso Rose's *Leave Me Alone*, and then left for home.

He knocked the door. As soon as it was opened, he said, "Dixie, I saw the original man, and I invited him to our wedding."

"Why don't you walk with your keys?"

"Because I know you'll always be here for me."

"Don't forget today is Bobby's birthday."

"I remember. I will be looking at Eldie's behavior and the way she's dressed."

"What will be wrong with her behavior and the way she would be dressed?"

"Lately, you attack me whenever I make a comment about my daughter as if my upbringing of her before you came was wrong."

"I know she's your daughter. I'm not attacking you. I just want you to be reasonable.

She's nineteen, and you brought her up well from the age of three months. As far as I know, her behavior in this house is sterling, and so it will be in Bobby's house. What do you expect it to be, dear Daddy?"

"Why are you mocking me?"

"Aren't you her dear Daddy?"

He didn't answer.

"But I'm her parent too since I've moved into the house overlooking Baisley Pond Park, the house that you sneaked out at nights and return when I'm fast asleep." She changed her tone. "My dear, I've put out your clothes for the party the way I, the yes woman, know. See how I'm always thinking of your welfare. Could you imagine how I'll be pampering you ten times ten when you put on that second ring on my finger?" She danced the floss.

Eldika walked in. "You are modern, Miss Dixie. I like those moves. But why are you flossing?"

"Because my eternal fiancé and I are going to Bobby's birthday party and we'll be flossing away."

Darwin raised his voice. “Dixie, don’t you go dancing with those under-aged children. You are a grown woman who should know your place.”

“Says who?”

Dixie purposely danced more, and wildly flossed.

“Miss Dixie, who taught you that new dance?” Eldika asked.

“Jaden Haye, the-seven-year-old kid who lives next door. I used to babysit him when his father, Samuel Haye, went to work with Delta at Kennedy.”

“Jaden taught you well. Now, come, Miss Dixie, and compete with me because dad said you cannot go by Bobby’s place and dance with the millennials because you are old.”

“Is that so?” Dixie said.

The two females flossed, flinging both hands at both sides of their bodies with fancy foot movements until Eldika got tired, stopped, and left. But Dixie continued with dirty dancing all around Darwin. She said, gyrating to the floor, and whispering, “My love, if you let

Eldie be herself at Bobby's party tonight, you'll get it on the bare floor where I can go deeper in for you to meet the pink of my pearl."

"I always wanted it on the floor so I'll let her be herself tonight with that white boy." He didn't whisper.

"Dad, stop describing white boy as leprosy." She came back from the kitchen.

"Eldie, I've told your father countless times to stop spitting in the air because one day his spit will fall in his face." Dixie spoke in disgust.

"Does the Flossing Doctrine put me on a hook?" Darwin appeared from nowhere.

"Yes, Sir Darwin. Be informed most anglers go out of their way to avoid hooking a shark...."

"Miss Sociologist, you are the shark or the hook?"

"Daddy and Miss Dixie, how come you two always catch fire without lightning flashing in your bedroom, in your bathroom, or anywhere for that matter? Is that black love with white sociology?"

He looked at Dixie. “I will be watching your behavior too.”

“Don’t worry, honey, I’ll be a nice girl. Let’s all have a small dinner. My mother taught me I should always have something in my stomach because the food served may be something I don’t eat.”

“You never told me how eight-year-old you and your mother survived when both of you were put out of the apartment for not paying rent and were homeless. What became of your mother?”

“She did not become a prostitute, if that is what you have been trying to find out for some time now. Her faith came through. She believed in the Almighty.”

“Did He come down from heaven and put you and mom in a big house?”

“Daily, I’m getting to know your mettle.”

“Woman, I already knew yours.”

“Dad and Miss Dixie, one of you must learn to walk away before lightning strikes.”

Darwin left to get dressed.

"Miss Dixie, guess what I bought as a gift for Bobby?"

"A box of condoms before he leaves for Harvard."

"No! No! No! You are so jovial."

"Eldie, I was using condoms from sixteen.

My mother packed my bag with three packs of the good kind of condoms when she sent me away to college. If I am, or not, married to your father, and I am in this house, I will pack your suitcase with four of the same pack of condoms that my mother put in my suitcase when you leave York to go to Harvard to meet Bobby. I used them and I didn't get pregnant or STDs." She put a comforting hand on Eldika's shoulders. "Girl, it's time for the ladies to get dressed to kill. I'm taking Michelle Obama's *Becoming* for Bobby's gift. He may learn something of other people's pain, other people's joy, other people's disappointments, and that we are all the same, whatever our color, our race, our religion, or our ethnicity. I want you to wear the Roberto Cavalli I bought for you. I went deep into my savings."

"Daddy doesn't want me to wear it."

"I promised him a gift, so he'll never object."

"What's that gift? Your eyes tell me to shut up."

"You have the eyes of a sociologist with that liberating experience in you."

"You studied sociology in college?"

"Yes."

"Which college?"

"College New Rochelle."

"My mother told me dad went there, and he dropped out early. And my father told me my mother went to that college too, and she dropped out early because she was having me. My mother also told me about all dad's bad ways."

"Like what?"

"Women. You know my mom when she was at that college?"

"Yes."

"As friends?"

"I was a senior. She was...." She stopped talking when she saw Darwin walking in on them.

"Ladies, how do I look?" Darwin pompously presented himself.

"Dad, great! Great!"

"Greater than great. Let's get married before we go to Bobby's party, Sir Darwin," Dixie said and laughed aloud.

They were now at the party, all dressed beautifully. Eldika left them, went into the ladies' room, changed her clothes, and remained in the ladies' room.

The party was crowded with folks of the millennial generation, of the silent generation, of generation X, and of the boomer generation. Nevertheless, there was mingling of all the generations—the young with the old; the old with the very old; the middle aged with the long-past middle aged; the wheel-chaired with their mobile spouses—a group devoid of ethnocentrism, only cultural relativity.

Dixie spoke in Darwin's ear. "This is how people should live. It is so nice of the Bradfords inviting us. Don't forget you'll have it on the floor tonight, but only with good behavior here."

"I won't give it to you if you pick up that old college flame, Harvey, if he's here, and you ignore me and fly away with him."

"The way I want that post-Bobby's romance on the floor, I'm not flying away with anyone before I get it, probably after."

The dancing stopped. Bobby moved to his cake and took up the knife on the table. The young ladies were giggling, shuffling, and pushing each other to get in front of the group in the same way President Trump pushed in the overseas summit to get in front of other dignitaries to have his picture taken. That was a shameful display of our President. The local summit was in the Bradford House and the girls wanted to get in the front tier so that Bobby will see them. Mrs. Bradford, who ruled Bobby's life, held Hillare Dieston's hand and walked her to a spot where nobody can block Bobby from seeing her. Dieston, an artificial blond, is beautiful, probably the most beautiful girl of her age in attendance. She wore a nicely fitting designer dress and her body displayed a recent suntan. Her strappy shoes showed her polished toes in the colors of the flag. She knew Mrs. Bradford loves the American flag as if the flag is her personal property, and Dieston meant to show Mrs. Bradford the flag she loves dearly is represented, not only on the pin on her designer dress.

Miriam Dixxon sneezed, and she was told to shut up instead of bless you.

Bobby's eyes were looking for someone in the bustling crowd, but that someone could not be seen. He was delaying the sticking of the cake until he sees that certain person come forward. But that certain person could not be seen. He was wondering if she came even though she had told him she'll surely be there whether there's a storm or a tsunami. He shouted aloud, "Eldika Wolmers, wherever you are hiding? Come forward and stick the cake with me." She came out of the ladies' room in a beanie hat and an over-sized sweater.

There were sighs, deep sighs, and the shocked face of Dixie's seeing Eldika had not worn the lovely dress she had bought for her at the Designer Block downtown Brooklyn. Neither Dixie nor Darwin knew when and where Eldika purchased her outfit. But Dixie knew Eldika wore that outfit to anger her father because when she, Dixie, was not around, she came to the conclusion Darwin must have told his daughter something uncomplimentary about the dress she, Dixie, bought.

Darwin spoke in Dixie's ear. "I'm going home."

"Eldie's daddy, you are staying here. If you pull your hand away, I'll scream." She hooked his right arm. He always complains his right arm hurts, and she held it firmly.

The crowd parted as the Red Sea as if Moses spoke when Eldika walked and styled her beanie the way Meghan Markle would have. She looked at her father and Miss Dixie, and, with a broad smile, bowed to them.

Dixie pulled Darwin closer to her and said, "Your daughter is going places. Leave her alone and success will be hers."

Bobby did not let Eldika walk the full distance by herself. He met her halfway, stopped in front of his mother, and hooked Eldika as his just-won Oscar prize. They stood side by side in front of the cake. The DJ, dressed like a clown, played *Somewhere Over The Rainbow*. Their knives pierced the cake and touched. They kissed gently on the lips and repeated the gentle kiss. The young people shouted, "The tongue! The tongue!" But Eldika and Bobby hugged as buddies, walked to the waxed floor and danced as the DJ mixed his music: Cardi

B's music for the floss and the dab dancers, and the 1970 music of Barry White singing *Baby, Baby* for the old timers.

Dixie released her hold on Darwin and he walked away. He was glad to walk farther away from her.

Two eyes met. Their stares penetrated each other with doubts and disbelief. Both moved forward.

"Dixie Boom Boom with two goat breasts!"

"Poonks who peeped at me in the bathroom to see my goat breasts!"

They hugged, embraced, laughed endlessly, but never kissed.

"What are you doing here, girl?"

"What are you doing here, boy?"

"Dixie, I'm a friend of the Bradfords. Oliver Bradford gave me a job when I came from the Navy. And you?"

"I came with my stepdaughter, Eldika, the girl who stuck the cake with Bobby. How is Aunt Ruby?"

"She retired from nursing and now lives in Florida, farming acres of navel oranges. She's rich, rich, rich."

"Do you remember what Aunt Ruby's advice was when we left for school every morning?"

"Let us say it together: If you fail to prepare, prepare to fail."

They did the tight fisted bump.

"Dixie Boom Boom, you said Eldika is your stepdaughter. When were you married?"

"I'm not married. I have been living with her father for some time now. Are you married, Poonks?"

"No; I am waiting for you. Then let's do some floss dancing."

"A little boy named Jaden, nicknamed Major, who lives on my block, taught me floss moves."

"The young lady I brought to the party taught me just yesterday. So let's do it. I know you will out-do me because you always danced for me when you wanted to sleep on the floor and let me go on the bed. You said then, 'It's your bed, and you should be sleeping on it.'"

They flossed away, Dixie improvising, gyrating beautifully with movements the millennials admired and cheered. Jason stepped aside and the crowd surrounded Dixie. Darwin was pissed to see her dancing so happily with a stranger and more pissed to see her gyrating movements that he only should be enjoying on the floor after the party. As much as Bobby had warned him if he hates politics he should keep away from the room with senior and very senior citizens. The room had a sign: SENIOR-SENIORS' POLITICS. BEWARE! In that room there were two men, and two women, well dressed, serving the seniors whatever they needed.

Darwin touched the door; a man opened it, and said, "Sir, you'll be served when you sit."

A woman said, "Darwin, Nina said we will be discussing politics soon, and, please, take a seat."

"Who are you? Who's Nina? How do you know my name?" He asked those three questions in one breath.

"My name is Marie; my job is to know

everyone who comes in this building and, especially who comes in this room. Nina is Mrs. Bradford who will let you know President Trump is the greatest President America ever had. She will be discussing tonight the negative things that the naysayers have been saying about our rich and truthful President. She will explain what the President really meant when he said those black people should go back to their infested countries they came from."

"Marie, your boss Nina doesn't know those four black women are Congresswomen, three are born here, and one is a Naturalized American." She did not answer. "And you are the yeast that makes Nina's political bread rise?"

She did not answer that question, but she said, "The usher will bring you two Make-America-Great-Again caps to make your choice. Those caps will show you to follow the vision of the greatest American President who ever lived."

"Marie, I'm going to get my wife, and both of us will take a seat. She will take the white MAGA cap, and I will take the dominant red because red is closer to black, and I am black who, up to this morning, had a senseless confrontation with a white guy."

"That white guy is not a Trumper. Followers of President Trump are fair and honest in all their dealings. Ignore that white fool. Take the caps now and wear them with pride for the world to see those caps make you an optimist as all Trumpians."

"When we come back singing *Joy to the World*, we will take the caps, Marie."

Darwin never returned.

He took a position and stood stoically where he can see the beautiful landscape and the garden of roses. He also saw the backs of Dixie and a man sitting close on the chairs in the garden. Eldika came to him and said, "Dad, Bobby wants to say something to you."

"Say it, Bobby."

"Mr. Darwin, it is so nice of you to come. I hope you enjoyed yourself and kept away from my mother's politics. Where is Miss Dixie? I want to thank her for Michelle Obama's *Becoming*."

"You'll find her enjoying the early foliage with a gentleman, Bobby." He pointed.

"Bobby, let's go and get her. I will go

home as soon as we find her." Eldika looked at her father, and he smiled gently.

Bobby made out Jason in the distance and shouted, "Jason! Jason! I didn't know you came to my party." Jason hugged him.

"You still pee your bed, Bobby? The large crowd blocked you from seeing me."

"Don't let people know that. Meet my BFF, Eldika Wolmers."

"Eldika, I am Jason."

"You are the little boy who called out to Aunt Ruby to take Dixie and her mother in." She paused. "And when Dixie wanted to sleep on the floor and let you sleep in your bed, she used to dance for you."

"You know my biography well."

"A humane one. I'm hoping Dixie marry my father. She's always putting off the date."

Dixie wanted that conversation about her impending wedding end, and she ended it. "Jason, we are leaving. It is so nice seeing you after all these years."

"Leaving so quickly? I will stay here a bit and chat with Bobby."

Bobby spoke. "Miss Dixie, thanks for your gift, Michelle Obama's *Becoming*. It is a beautiful book. I'm in the chapter where Michelle's feelings came rushing for Barack and she had a toppling blast of lust for him."

"Bobby, you are a speed reader. You and I must discuss all what Michelle Obama wrote in her true story."

"I will."

Dixie kissed Bobby's left cheek; Eldika kissed the right.

Jason said, "What about my cheeks, ladies?"

Dixie and Eldika kissed Jason cheeks, ran, and giggled.

Darwin waited in the car and said immediately as they sat, "Eldika, why you put on those ugly clothes?"

"Dad, I had a nice time. Please, don't start. You said what Miss Dixie bought for me is whorish. Let us go home in love."

"Eldie, when he told you that dress is ho-ish?" Dixie asked.

She did not answer.

"I'd bet the phone will ring late tonight," Darwin said with a tone of certainty as a true prophet.

"Not for me," Eldika answered. "I told Bobby we'll talk in the break at college tomorrow."

The séance people call it goat mouth. The phone rang one minute after midnight. "Hello," Dixie said.

"Aunt Ruby's boy's calling."

"Talk tomorrow. Goodnight." She hung up.

"Who's that calling your phone so late?"

"Darwin, do I ask questions when your phone rings at late hours with the tune Lover, come back to me?"

"Soon it will be ringing, The end of a love affair." He turned his face to the wall and went to bed. His snoring echoed.

At the dinner table next morning Eldika asked, "Dad, why are you so cold with Miss Dixie?"

"Why are you always picking up for that woman?"

"That woman has a name!" Dixie shouted.

Eldika said, "What's going on with you two since we came from Bobby's party last night?"

"He lost his bet," Dixie said.

"What was that bet, Miss Dixie?" Eldika asked.

"You are no longer a child. Ask, dear daddy. He will tell you about the interesting bet we made and he lost."

"Probably another time, I will ask him, Miss Dixie. Daddy doesn't take losses kindly."

"Girl, I found that out."

The once harmonious household was no longer a home of happy family conversations, bickering times prevailed. Darwin left in the morning for work, returned late at nights, and Dixie did not know his whereabouts after work. He was accustomed to call and ask what to bring home for dinner. That habit ended. Dixie followed suit. But when she left home she was with Jason. First, she returned home after two hours; then it became after three hours; then it became late at nights with Uber bringing her home, not public transport. Her interest grew for, and increased for, Jason. She asked herself: Is it love, sweet memories, or gratitude? But she didn't care for an answer.

One night when she went to bed with Darwin hugging his pillow, his back turned to her, and his loud snoring annoyed her, she went to the spare room, and she retraced her full life as a little girl, especially the day she and her mother were tired and hungry, as they paced the streets of Brooklyn on that humid day looking for a place to live after the landlord evicted them. Her thoughts strayed to their journey which began from Foster and Bedford Avenues to Avenue U, and from Avenue U they walked east on Batchelder Street. Then they rested with their bundles and gazed around.

Again she imagined that vivid memory of a little boy, five years old, who rode his bicycle out of his yard and she said to him, "My mother and I are hungry and homeless, you know of anybody who can help us?"

He braked on his bicycle and said, "Ask Aunt Ruby. She helps everybody." Seeing they stood still as a pole buried in cement, the little boy dropped his bicycle, rushed upstairs and told his Aunt Ruby a woman and her child have a big problem.

"Jason, tell them to come inside."

He rushed back. "Two of you, Aunt Ruby says to come inside."

"Are you sure?" I smiled, happiness overwhelmed me.

"I'm sure, sure. Aunt Ruby helps everybody."

"My name is Dixie. What's your name?"

"Jason." As they walked inside and Aunt Ruby welcomed the strangers warmly, Jason said, "Aunt Ruby, let Dixie stay in my room and sleep on my bed. I will sleep with my comforter on the floor."

Dixie remembers she shouted as if she's Jason's big sister, "No, no, Jason! I will sleep on the floor. It's your bed; you are a little boy, so you should sleep on it."

Her memories became alive remembering Aunt Ruby laughed aloud, hugged Jason and her, and told her mother, "Florence, my home is yours and your daughter's as long as both of you wish."

Thunder burst in the sky, lightning flashed through the room, she woke up from her dream, tears dripped on her pillow, and she uttered the words, "Thank you, Jason. I love you. Aunt Ruby, I'll always be grateful to you."

CHAPTER 5

Darwin left the house without saying a word to Dixie. Dixie dressed after he left. She wore a floral green, self-portrait dress that she styled with a smart Alexander McQueen blazer and Manolo Blahnik pumps. She had saved her money for two years to afford this attire which was for her wedding to take place at City Hall next month. She called Jason. "Poonks, can you take me some place today, any place, even to hell, to let the devil burn me for my sins being in love with you?"

"Dixie Boom Boom, are you wearing clean drawers?"

"I have the bloomers Aunt Ruby left drying on the clothes line."

"You washed it?"

"What's that stuff Aunt Ruby used to wash her clothes?"

"Dettol."

"Yes; I used that stuff."

"Can I take it off to smell it?"

"Where?"

"In my show tonight."

"Where is that show?"

"Comedy Central in Manhattan."

"Jason, you are a comedian?"

"That's how I got money before going into the Navy."

"When was that?"

"Since you moved away and hid your address from Aunt Ruby and me."

"I thought Aunt Ruby wanted you to be somebody."

"Isn't comedian a noun?"

"Yes."

"Well, somebody is a common noun, and I am that proper noun at Comedy central."

"Mr. Somebody, I'm dressed with Victoria's secrets below, and I will sin if I take them off, but I don't mind taking them off for you tonight. Where should I meet you?"

"The same place you left me last night."

"That will be too emotional to meet you there again."

"Well, take Uber, and meet me at Comedy Central in Manhattan. If I am not there to greet you, ask for Totohead."

"What kind of name is that?"

"That's my stage name, and someone will know you are my guest and will seat you in the front row to applaud me to the top of your lungs for all my jokes."

"I'll be there, Totohead."

The show began promptly at 10 pm. The first three comedians brought cheers to the crowd, but when the name Totohead was announced, the noisy audience never ended their tremendous applause until the Master of Ceremonies begged them to stop by lowering both hands to the floor. With the noises still raging, Dixie looked at the audience's attires in sweats, in sneakers, in dirty jeans, in over-sized slippers, in caps with peaks turned south, south east, and southwest, and women with ugly legs in shorts. She asked herself, Why was she in such a place wearing the clothes she bought to be married next month? She took off her blazer and sat on it.

Totohead walked in to renewed noises: "Totohead! Totohead! Totohead!"

He began: "There's a woman in the audience from Ascot, England; she's sitting on her Alexander McQueen blazer; she slipped on her way home to Ascot. The cabby called out for her as a passenger, 'Ascot, madam?' She shouted, 'Slightly bruised.'"

The crowd shouted, "What she bruised?" They laughed vulgarly, and said, "Where is that Ascot broad who bruised her arse sitting?"

Totohead gave jokes nonstop for forty five minutes, and the crowd burst into laughter at each joke. He ended with this joke: "Sons and daughters of you fuckin bitches, I witnessed what I'm going to tell youse with my two blue eyes and a new pair of spectacles on them."

"Totohead, your eyes isn't blue," a man shouted.

"Arsehole, when you went to work your wife told me she loves my blue eyes. Ask her when you go home if I didn't sleep on the bed with the inner spring mattress."

The crowd laughed at the man.

A Jamaican shouted, "Whey the fuck you was told you have blue eyes?"

"Illegal immigrant, people in your shit-hole country told me so. Leave now before I tell Trump and his ICE PEOPLE about you, and to send your ass back to your shit-hole country. Trump says your fuckin country is infested. Is that so?" The crowd laughed heartily, and Totohead continued. "An American tourist on vacation in that illegal immigrant's country named Jamaica, looked up a coconut tree and saw a teenaged girl picking coconut without a panty on. The tourist waited until the little girl got down from the coconut tree and gave her twenty dollars to buy a panty. Her mother, Agnes, a trickster, saw what took place. The next day Agnes saw the American tourist walking her way. She rushed up the same coconut tree, and as the tourist looked up, she quickly slid down the coconut tree. The tourist gave her one dollar, and said, 'Woman, buy a hair net to cover all those gray hairs. They are disgusting.'"

The crowd went wild. Jason took Dixie on stage, introduced her to the noisy audience, and said, "This is the little girl who climbed up the coconut tree in Jamaica without a panty and got twenty dollars from the American tourist."

"She really looks like a tomboy in frills," a man said and laughed alone.

"Where's her mudder with those gray hairs?" an old man with a bald head asked.

"West Indian Jamaican, in my appearance tomorrow, I'll bring her mudder for you to smell the hair net, and then you can use the hair net to strain your peas and rice when you cook Sunday dinner for your greedy guests who hate cooking."

"I already told him I'll give him my net to smell," a Trini woman said.

People were teasing each other in their own sidebars.

The show ended noisily.

As Jason got in his car to take Dixie home, she said, "Those are all Aunt Ruby's jokes that you recycled. Shame on you!"

"Shakespeare stole people's lines and became famous; I borrowed Aunt Ruby's jokes to make a living when I was broke; and today I use them to get money for you. What's the big deal?"

"The big deal is I don't need your Comedy Central money. My man gives me Chase Bank money. Why didn't you bring to Comedy Central the white woman you brought to Bobby's birthday party so you can introduce her to that nasty crowd?"

"I brought you so that we can start over with nasty loving that Aunt Ruby did not want us to do when we were children."

"I have a man, and I'm wearing his engagement ring. I'm even wearing the clothes I'm supposed to get married in, to him, next month."

"Then why are you wearing those clothes today?"

"Believe me, I don't know why."

"Both of you had a big quarrel?"

"We have been quarrelling for weeks."

"Because of me?"

"Yes; because of you and our dirty dancing, and you calling me late at nights when we are in bed and making love. Let's not talk about that."

"What can we talk about?"

"Memories."

"Like what?"

"In all my life, I've never met a person as your Aunt Ruby—she took my mother and me in, fed us, gave my mother a job...Up to last night I cried thinking of her kindness, and I've never gone back to see her since I left. Isn't that a shame? And, of course, your words that live in my brain: Ask Aunt Ruby. She helps everybody."

"What is bothering you about my words?"

"My ingratitude."

"You are crying. Then you can visit Aunt Ruby before or after your marriage."

In the back seat of his car, Jason went close to her, and hugged her gently. She rested her head on his shoulder, looked in his eyes, their lips touched, parted, and deep kissing began, continuously.

"Jason, this shouldn't happen."

"Why?"

"I'm going to get married soon."

"Let me take you home."

"No. I'll call Uber. And don't call me again, please. You did it twice when my man and I were fuckin."

"I obeyed you when we were children, and I will continue to obey you now and forever. I promise."

"Thanks, Poonks, for not forcing me to be sexual as much as I wanted you to do it in your car."

"Is that so?"

"One hundred percent true."

He started singing, *We'll be together*

again.... She rushed into Uber without looking back but mumbling to herself: I've got to try to be nice to Darwin. There's no future with Jason. He helped me once. That's past tense; I've got to live in the present with Darwin. Being the wife of a comedian without an audience for many days is not good enough for me. Without an audience is going to be without money, without food, without health care. Wisdom is whispering to me now, and I have to think.

She looked back continuously.

"Do you want to go back, Miss?" the cabby asked, and stopped.

"No. Here's your money. Goodnight."

CHAPTER 6

Dixie woke up next morning, set the table, made a sumptuous breakfast—scrambled eggs without the albumen, with slices of ham, with green and red sweet peppers, with diced onions, with a tip of salt, with a tip of black pepper, and fried in no other oil but Goya's. "Darling," she called.

Shocked, he did not answer, until he heard, "Darwin darling, don't let your coffee get cold."

He answered, "I'll be right there, my love." He looked at the table decorated with all the wares and cutlery only seen on their first day of sharing the house overlooking the Baisley Pond Park. He walked to the chair on which he usually sits.

"That's Eldie's chair now. You'll sit next to me where we can touch each other's leg, touch between my legs, and you will know I'm not wearing a panty." She poured his coffee. "Don't tell me; I know how many spoonfuls of sugar you need. And you'll get my sugar on the floor as I'd promised you after Bobby's birthday. Let's raise our cups to a lasting friendship because friendship comes first, and our early marriage which will be next and permanent."

"Sure."

"Darwin, you showed no enthusiasm."

"Sure! Sure, my love."

"Honey, that more sounds like enthusiasm. What do you think is the reason for our strained relationship all these past months?"

"My fault, Dixie."

"No; it's my fault, Darwin."

They touched their coffee cups, and said in unison, "Our stupidity." Then Darwin blurted, "This is the year you told me we'd get married. Have you picked the month?"

"That year has come really quickly." She looked at him with a broad smile.

"I thought that year would have never come. In the wee hours of the past mornings, I thought of when that day would come."

"I wore the Meghan Markle outfit yesterday."

"I noticed."

"You noticed?"

"Yes; I noticed."

"You left here very early yesterday while I was showering, and when I came in last night, you were locked in the spare room, and snoring. When did you notice that I wore the Meghan Markle outfit?"

"From the day you bought that outfit and said that's the dress you'd get married in at City Hall, every morning I look at that dress and the exact spot it is hanging, when we fight, when we make love, when I leave the house, when I didn't speak to you, when I come home, before I go to bed, and that became my insane habit, my MO, my *modus operandi*. Do you believe me?"

"Yes," she said softly.

He repeated every word he said before.

"Yes; I believe you, Darwin."

"Can I ask why you wore that beautiful dress yesterday?" He looked at her. "You don't have to answer. I don't have a pink slip to fire you; neither would I ever have one for you. You are the one with pink slips." He smiled, and pinched her below her dress. "I've realized my way of showing who I am without knowing who you are was the wrong way. Eldie spoke to me of my stupidity and my bullying ways towards you. But she also spoke of your changed and suspicious behavior too."

"Darwin, my love, I will tell you why I wore my wedding outfit...." She paused. "You have been leaving the house after I put breakfast on the table, ignoring me and my breakfast with all the ingredients you like, slamming the door and driving away. During those mornings my mind traveled backwards to a time when my homeless mother and I asked a little boy named Jason where can we get a place to live—the words of this little boy still linger in my thoughts—'Ask Aunt Ruby...She helps everybody.' I dressed up to meet that little boy. He's three years my junior."

"That was he that you were sitting closely

with in the garden?"

"Yes."

"If you marry me, I'll never stop loving you, and I'd want you to wear that same Meghan Markle outfit on our wedding day."

"Why?"

"First, every solution to a problem starts with a discussion, and that is what we are doing now. Second, when you had tried on that dress and had asked me how do you look, you remember what I had told you?"

"Of course!"

"Now, do you still wish to marry me as early as possible, or do you prefer to wait a little?"

She looked at him, somewhat sternly. "Darwin, you are making your love for me a kind of algorithm—step by step."

"That's your MO, and you do it very often."

Eldika walked in. "Dad and Miss Dixie, I see both of you are on good terms again. I like that. Please, let it last longer than that blood wolf moon over New York." She looked at them, but addressed Dixie. "Daddy told me this is the year you'd marry him. When is that day?" She didn't wait for Dixie to answer when Darwin excused himself, but he stood still within hearing distance. "Miss Dixie, for a very long time, Dad had been showing me your Meghan Markle outfit that he looks at every night. Now I'm twenty one, can we talk?"

"Let me clear the table first."

Darwin moved completely away from the table and out of their way. "Ladies, I think I'll find my way down to the beautiful institution called Baisley Pond Park. In that institution people of many nations 'jog in the park to lessen their fat, and you should do that too, Ma.' I once heard a teenager say that to her mother. But today Dixie and I will be in the barbecuing section of the park cooking. You can join us, Eldie."

"Won't you be seeing A'Ferti today to discuss the American Indian's life, daddy?"

"Of course. I'll be there with him for a long time to give you and Miss Dixie sufficient time to discuss which month she'd marry me. It's now the beginning of another summer."

"We'll meet you there, dad." As soon as Darwin left, she said, "Miss Dixie hand me the dishes you washed; I'll dry them so we can speed up and have our discussion before dad returns."

"If I'm not here, you'd help your father dry the dishes?"

"Where are you going? Aren't you going to marry before the summer ends?"

"I don't know."

"What you mean by saying you don't know, Miss Dixie?"

"Jason has been calling me, and I've been seeing him."

"What! Dad has dropped his bad habits of leaving the house early in the morning and coming home late at nights. Why can't you stop your bad habits of seeing Jason? Do you owe him a lifetime Thank you for rescuing you and your mother from homelessness?"

Their eyes clashed: Eldika's were bold; Dixie's were weak. The dishwashing and drying process was finished. Dixie held Eldika's hand firmly, led her to the bedroom, locked it, and they sat on the bed. Both were silent, both shuffled their legs and played with their fingers. Finally, Eldika spoke. "You are in love with him?"

"Who?"

"Jason, and with both of them."

"What do you mean by with both of them?"

"With Darwin and Jason. What Jason does for his living?" She only pursued the last question.

"He's a comedian."

"A fuckin comedian!"

"Yes; a fuckin comedian!"

"You'd be leaving my father, salaried, with a pension, social security, and with a sizable savings at Chase Bank?"

"Who said I'm leaving him?"

"There's going to be a three-some in bed?"

"What! Repeat what you said."

"You heard me. Can I leave now?"

"You may. But it will be so nice to listen to what I have to say because soon you may be in that same position: The young man you love to hear recite the poem *If* may not be the same person you'd love forever without interruptions."

"Who'd be in your life forever—Dad or Jason without interruptions?" She opened the bedroom door as she heard a noise.

The front door is pushed opened with a loud noise. "A'Ferti confirms he will be the best man in the wedding. Say hurrah, ladies."

"Hurrah!"

"Hurrah!"

"Ladies, let's get ready to go barbecuing by the pond, not where the Guyanese flock with their loud tassa drums and disturb the peace and tranquility of the park."

Dixie said, "Darwin Wolmers, change your tone and the way you match your words."

"What's wrong with what I say?"

"You are ethnocentric believing your

Trini culture is what others should be obeying. You are behaving as President Trump who hates Muslims—for that matter, he hates black people in general. He loves himself and his golden hair."

Eldika sensed a fight with words could break out between them. "Dad, every morning when you wake up greet Miss Dixie with a kiss and tell her you love her."

Dad held Dixie, danced, and sang in her ear, *Before you came into my life nothing went right.*

"That's so true, Mr. Wolmers."

"Let's get married in June, my love," he sang.

"Please, change that tune."

"Why, my dear?"

"I prefer July or August, better still September or October when it is cool outside." Her cell rings, a strange voice, a strange caller calls. "Excuse me, Darwin."

He and Eldika walked away.

"Hello," Dixie answered.

"Totohead's calling his little sister."

"I told you to stop calling me!"

"You always wanted to see Aunt Ruby. I bought two Delta airline tickets for us to fly to a romantic place called Florida."

"You think I'll leave my good life to go and live with a comedian. Aunt Ruby told you to do something worthwhile. You call what you do is something worthwhile that will please Aunt Ruby and me?"

"Yes."

"Making nasty jokes about women, and calling me, a decent woman, on stage to close your show with vulgar jokes, are things worthwhile?"

"That's called moonlighting."

"What do you mean?"

"I work with a Fortune 500 Electric Company in New York as a CPM, and I'm transferred to Florida as a higher paid CPM."

"What!"

"As a CPM."

"As a Cunt and Prick Man! Since you were a teenager you had been trying to get under my skirt to be the first CPM who laid me when I was changing my clothes in the bathroom."

Jason's laughter came through her phone as loud as a fire brigade siren. "You can open my show in downtown Miami next to the famous Versace building."

"I don't want to open any fuckin show with you! Goodbye!" She cut him off.

Immediately, he texted her with words that he thinks would convince her:

Dixie Boom Boom, when we met at Bobby's birthday party, I was a CPM; and CPM means Customer Project Manager. In a nutshell, I manage all facets of a project to completion within budget in a given timeline. My pay is great. The yearly bonus is great. But the high level of stress without you at my side will be greater than the money in my pocket. Big sister, your little brother needs you to manage his money and his careless living. Aunt Ruby told me to call you and ask you to marry me.

He continues his text to Dixie:

Aunt Ruby is a smart woman. Dixie Boom Boom, I'm sure you remember this: Those two fuckin Italian women were always saying nasty things about you in Italian about your black color; but they always say the N word in English. Aunt Ruby, after her RN duties in Mount Sinai Hospital, would stay up late at nights and learn Italian from books, records, and quietly from the Italian mailman. When the mailman dropped the mail, Aunt Ruby called him inside, gave him a drink, and practiced her Italian with him. He corrected her diction and grammar; and she gave him a Christmas envelope every year for two years.

Big sister, I'm sure you'll remember this incident: The mailman was about to climb the step to come for his drink. Aunt Ruby had already taken off the alarm for him to come in, but she saw those two Italian-American gossipers as prey eaters at their boundaries talking and delivering the N word like an award to you. Aunt Ruby shouted to the mailman, 'Robert, I am busy today. Leave my mail on the step. I just learned a sacred aria that Renee Fleming sings with Luciano Pavarotti.' Her every word was Italian with the correct diction and grammar. That was her bait to draw the mailman into a long conversation.

"Ruby, sing it for me." Robert spoke Italian.

"Sure," she answered in Italian.

"I will lawn your grass if you sing the Italian Anthem instead." He was kidding.

"For sure, I will not sing it with those two peasants' accent. Batchelder/Avenue U has two peasants who call me and my little girl by the N word." She sang. Her voice was clear; her ribbon of tone was perfect; and he joined her to the end of the Italian Anthem.

Aunt Ruby spoke louder. "Robert, by your diction, I can see you were never a peasant in Italy. Those two bitches at their fence were, I'm sure, very poor peasants with dirt below their broad fingers digging potatoes for dinner. Don't come to cut my lawn." She spoke Italian slowly, and she had her reason for doing so.

Jason answers a telephone call, and he continues typing his text:

Dixie Boom Boom, you remember both women at their boundaries went inside. Less than a month later, one sold her house and left Batchelder Street. The other at the corner of Avenue U never came outside to collect her mail from the mailman. Her habit changed: She got a contractor to construct a mailbox on her boundary fence.

You remember at nights, we mocked Aunt Ruby faking the Italian language as if we were the two fuckin Italian women who congregated at their boundaries. Every night Aunt Ruby sent us to bed with a proverb. Her proverb to us the nights we mocked her was, Chil-ren, let people buy you for a fool, but don't let them sell you for a fool.

Dixie's eyes were transfixed on Jason's text; and her tears dripped.

My dear Dixie Boom Boom, let me stop fooling around and tell you a little more of the job that I will be taking up at Power and Light in Florida: My duties as a CPM include consulting, assisting in design, meeting with engineers, architects, clients, electricians, and trades, to coordinate my team and their workers' collective efforts.

Big sister, please, come. We'll travel together to a romantic land called Florida, and we'll relive all the proverbs of Aunt Ruby's life and ours. Delta gave discounted tickets for two. Be there 1600 hours, sharp, because I must catch that flight today to fill that new job appointment tomorrow.

I love you from the day five-year-old me said to you: Ask Aunt Ruby. She helps everybody. Believe me, Dixie Boom Boom, from that hot, summer day that I first saw you, you have been MY EVERYTHING up to today. (His text ends).

Dixie read the last paragraph of that text over and over. Her tears dripped heavily, and her life changed from being the future wife of Darwin to being whatever Jason wants her to be.

Eldika interrupted her thoughts and prevented her from re-reading Jason's text. Dixie ran into her bedroom, dried her tears, and returned into the living room.

"Miss Dixie, we are packed for the barbecuing in the park. And we are hot! What is delaying you?" she shouted.

Dixie wanted to lie and say she has a bad headache and to go and leave her. But she said in a convincing voice, "Eldie, I was changing into park clothes to be more comfortable." Eldika left. Dixie read again, Ask Aunt Ruby...She helps everybody. She didn't get into Juilliard's because she refused to go even though Aunt Ruby was willing to sponsor her, but her acting was superb to hide her inner sadness when her mind went in reverse. Her love for Jason catapulted Darwin's true love for her. She remembered getting off the bed and sleeping on the floor with Jason. They hugged; they pinched each other in the bottom, sometimes she had no panty because she wet it and took it off; and she liked when Jason pinched her when she had on no panty. They'd use each other's toothbrush; they'd rush to the dining table, and they'd mock Aunt Ruby's Jamaican bugle calls: "Chil-ren, chil-ren, come and eat. I have to be at Mount Sinai Hospital early today because I'm in the operating ward." Aunt Ruby replied with the same line every time, "Your chil-ren will mock you too when you get old and uglier than I."

Once Jason asked, "Aunt Ruby, how we will have children when we are children?"

"When you get big," Aunt Ruby said.

Dixie, three years older than Jason and thinks she's smarter than he, said, "Jason is my little brother. I won't marry him."

Jason spoke quickly. "We sleep together, so we can marry. Aunt Ruby and Uncle Roy sleep together because they are married."

Eldika returned and shouted angrily to Dixie who was singing and thinking solemnly of the past.

"Miss Dixie, we are burning up in the car waiting for you. I come back to get you, and you are singing along with Sarah Vaughan *In A Sentimental Mood.* I know the words of that song. It is a woman wishing she had the man of her choice in her bed. Your choice is not my father. You have been advising me about life, but I have been noticing you and your hypocrisy. Since you got that call twenty minutes ago you have changed as a chameleon. And I know who called you. My father has changed for the better because he loves you. When he left the house every morning and was not talking to you, he was not going into another woman's arm. He was going to work, and after work he hanged out with Aunt Doreen. Dixie, you are still in love with Jason. When you left home, I am sure you went to get laid by Jason. Isn't that true?"

Dixie did not answer her. She ran to the car, sat in the front seat next to Darwin, and kissed him.

Eldika coughed and coughed seeing Dixie pretense.

"You need a cough syrup, Eldie?" Darwin asked.

"You should buy a cough syrup based

with truth serum for a certain woman, dad."

Darwin did not ask her why and for whom. Dixie put her hand around his neck, and he said, "Dixie, I see you are wearing cargo pants. What's the occasion?"

"Honey, I'm wearing cargo pants because I am celebrating fifty years today of John Carlos and Tommy Smith's raised fists, their black-power fists to demand black power should be observed. I'm also celebrating the year of first meeting you in Baisley Pond Park, and the first sunny day of having barbeque with you in this community park where you met A'Ferti and looked at the beautiful women in their panty shorts."

"On a scale of one to ten, how would you grade our living together and courtship?"

"Six."

He looked at her expecting a higher grade as he parked the car on Rockaway Avenue.

Eldika spoke, but she chose her words, changed her tone and behavior, and she purposely left out Dixie's name. "Dad, have you chosen a date for that imaginary wedding?"

"My Princess, since we are all here together—that has not happened for a long time—we should choose a date conducive to all parties."

"Dad, exempt me from your discussion of choosing an imaginary date." She moved away, sat on a bench by herself, and sang *In A Sentimental Mood* to the top of her voice, but she improvised on the words including snake and poison as her favorite common nouns. Dixie alone busied herself in the food-preparation ordeal.

It was a warm and lovely day in early October. The circle around the pond was filled with joggers, slow and fast walkers, people in golf carts, caregivers and their clients, and the same group of Japanese joggers with procedure masks that covered their nostrils and mouths moved merrily along. A Trini steelband played calypsos and celebrated the fifty seventh year of The Republic of Trinidad and Tobago Independence. The band was crowded; the participants enjoyed themselves, and sang a medley of calypsos. A beautiful Trini woman in panty shorts, her shapely legs creamed, waved a Trini flag in front of the cheering crowd. Dixie had her cargo pants packed with certain things and wanted to use the opportunity to go dancing in the steelband, and when the steelband was out of Eldika and Darwin's sight, she'd leave it, call Jason, and tell him that she's on her way to him. Her thought was interrupted when Darwin said, "What can I serve my future wife?"

"Honey, sit. I will serve you. You want fish, beef, or chicken?"

"Mix them with plenty veggies. I want to cut down my belly before my wedding date."

"Should I serve you this lovely barbeque in a horse-to-a-rabbit proportion?" She smiled.

"In the same proportion you served Harvey."

"You just spoiled my fuckin day. I'm leaving."

"Honey, that's a joke."

"That's no fuckin joke to me."

"Dixie, I apologize. Please, don't leave. I'm leaving next week to fill a short appointment for the bank in Florida. I didn't tell you about it because I wanted to surprise you later tonight that I'm taking you with me. How do you like my surprise packet?"

Her eyes opened wide.

"Say something, Dixie."

"Like what?"

"You want to go or you don't want to go?"

All she thought of was when wisdom whispers what she should say. But at that moment no one was whispering wisdom in her ear—neither the wind, neither the overhead sun, nor the ducks in the pond; nobody was. She thought: Is this the place I choose to die because of my love for two men? Aunt Ruby had told her before she left home that she should never have any man's problem. He should have his own problem and bear them by himself.

A slow walking individual came closer and closer until his full body was visible. Darwin shouted, "A'Ferti, A'Ferti!"

"Yes, yes, my friend."

"A'Ferti, come and meet my beautiful fiancé that I've spoken to you about so many mornings in this park."

A'Ferti recited his full name to greet Dixie. "I'm honored to meet you, sister."

"Please, share in our barbeque," Dixie said.

"How do you know I am hungry, sister?"

"My brother, you are hungry for my barbeque, and I am hungry to know how you became white."

"Didn't your fiancé tell you?" He was about to tell her.

"Not now, A'Ferti."

Eldika moved from the bench where she sat and now sat on one of the chairs they brought. She put her chair next to A'Ferti.

"You are very pretty. What's your name?" A'Ferti asked.

"Eldika Wolmers. I see you from my window many mornings. Do you exercise in the park regularly?"

"Yes, I do. Your father speaks highly of you."

"What he tells you about me?"

"You graduated from college and you are seeking employment."

Darwin was about to put the slice of fish on the fork he held into his mouth, but he rested the fork down. "Dixie, I've never seen you check your cell so often to know the time. You have someone to meet soon?" It was 2:00 pm.

"I'm waiting for the Trini steelband to come around to go in the band and dance. At college, there was a Trini students' steelband, and I played the tenor pan."

"You never told me that before. I heard Harvey is a Trini. You are going to look for him to do your dirty dancing as the flag woman in the beret?"

She wanted to curse Darwin with the nastiest Trini Ebonics she learned from Trini people at college, but A'Ferti was in their company. Somehow Aunt Ruby's last words of advice before she left Aunt Ruby's home on Batchelder Street and Avenue U came to mind: Dixie Dunkirk, when wisdom whispers take heed. Wisdom whispers in us when we are confronted in adversity. Dixie felt she must take heed with patience and hoped the Trini steelband comes around quickly. She never looked at her cell again, but she was calculating every minute in her mind that passed as she addressed A'Ferti. "A'Ferti,"she rattled his full name, "what makes you a white male?"

He looked at her. "You know my name better than most."

“A’Ferti, she has an ax to grind, and that is why she had been practicing it,” Eldika said, and looked at Dixie sternly. Her hatred for Dixie was overt.

“For what purpose she has an ax to grind, Eldika?” A’Ferti asked.

Dixie didn’t wait for Eldika to answer. “For selfishness, A’Ferti! I am waiting to go dancing in the Trini steelband, but I am anxious to hear you speak in glowing terms of your Cherokee people.”

“Ladies and gentleman, it’s a long time I haven’t had such a delicious lunch. I can eat some more and take home a doggie bag.”

Dixie rushed to share him another plate as she heard the music of the Trini steelband quickly approaching.

Darwin asked all the questions he shouldn’t ask Dixie in the company of A’Ferti. But his daughter had two axes to grind, and she wanted A’Ferti to hear the main ax that needed grinding.

Dixie called A’Ferti’s full name again because she knew he liked his full name to be called. But she also knew he hates to be called

Sir; and that's how she called him when the Trini steelband was upon them. The flag woman in front of the band was holding and spinning the pole of the flag with dexterity with one hand and gyrating to the ground at the same time. She was cheered loudly by onlookers.

"Sister, let me tell you what the letters in the word S.I.R means."

"Brother, tell me when I come back after dancing to this Trini music." Dixie dropped her dish and rushed out.

Eldika rushed behind her and shouted: "Liar! Snake! I know you are not coming back. I hope you catch the 1600 hours flight to be out of my sight permanently. Begin getting laid in Delta to show the pilot what a slut you are. Sweet riddance, bitch."

Dixie knew her cover was blown, but she pretended she didn't hear Eldika. She rushed to meet the steelband, and she danced in the middle of the crowd till she reached 119th Avenue. She rushed up the avenue and stopped at the business address that read 118-11 Sutphin Street, Queens, New York. It was 3.20 p.m. She stopped a road two-dollar-a-passenger taxi. "Driver, take me to Kennedy to Delta to catch the four o'clock flight. Here's fifty dollars. I'll give you fifty more if I catch my flight."

"Miss, the traffic is blocked on Rockaway Avenue because of an accident. But I will do my best. Why so late? You were in your flower garden working hard in` your cargo pants on?"

"Get me there. Forget how I look and what I'm wearing."

"I'll do my best, lady."

His best was not good enough. She lost the 1600 flight and shouted to the clerk at Delta desk, "This is a day in the life of a fool!" She stood and wondered if she rushed for the shadow in the water and let the bone in her mouth fall, another one of Aunt Ruby's Jamaican nightly proverbs to Jason and her.

She called Uber. Uber came and asked if she is Dunkirk. She said yes. Uber said, "Dunkirk, this is a shared ride. I have to pick up another person at Jet Blue."

"Man or woman?"

"I don't know, Dunkirk."

"I was in my flower garden. I have on my boyfriend's cargo pants, and I feel dirty. I hope that person is not Charlize Theron in Givenchy Haute Couture."

"I don't know."

"Is it a man or a woman?"

"I don't know."

"What's the person's name?"

"Cocoa Panyol."

"What kind of name is that?"

"I know the exact spot that person says to wait. I will wait no longer than sixty seconds for this so-called Cocoa Panyol."

Uber stopped, looked at his watch, and in less than a minute a man knocked his door, and asked, "Are you Hamid?"

"Yes. Are you Cocoa Panyol?"

"Yes. Unlock your door for me."

"Your seat is in the back on the left side, Cocoa Panyol. Someone is on the right side."

"I hope that someone is not a fat one to take up two seats," Cocoa Panyol said before

Hamid unlocked the car door.

Dunkirk's voice had become sharp, almost strident when she looked at him and answered. "Cocoa Panyol, I hope there's enough space for your aged and swiveled body. You are an insensitive son of a bitch! It is time to give back some of your World War II age to mark a tombstone in Long Giland. You are the kind of brown nigga who thinks you are better than black me. Why am I in this fuckin Uber? I want to scream having to sit next to this old dick with a bucket hat and who is the same age with Methuselah."

"Hamid, stop the car!" Cocoa Panyol shouted.

"Why?" Hamid asked.

"Hamid, the old man wants to pee-pee," Dixie shouted.

"Cocoa Panyol, you want to piss?" Hamid asked.

"No! I want to throw away this bucket hat to be less old than Methuselah."

Hamid asked, "Who the hell is that old dude?"

Dixie answered. "He is a very, very, old Jewish man in the bible who is not as old as the fuckin bitch with the bucket hat."

Hamid stopped the car; Cocoa Panyol came out, walked a distance of three yards away from the car, and threw his bucket hat as far as he could. He looked at Dixie, and asked, "Miss, I still look as old as Methuselah?"

"Yes, just minus your sweaty bucket hat."

"Miss, you gave me the correct answers for my insensitive remark. And I apologize for my behavior. I just had a fight with a man."

"He is your youthful age?"

He smiled and stretched his hand. "What your name, may I ask?"

"Dixie Dunkirk. Was that man fat as I?"

"Ms. Dunkirk, you are no heavier than one hundred pounds."

"One twenty five."

"You are the same weight as my daughter who lives in Maryland. Hamid, please, put on the light to let me see if this one-hundred-twenty-five-pound beauty is prettier than any of my daughters."

It was daylight, but Hamid turned on the light over their heads.

"Hamid, she's prettier than all my daughters. I am sure she was compensated for her birth and beauty by the angels. She can live in my brownstone when she grows up to be a woman. I live in the basement, and my other floors are empty since my wife died. I am afraid to rent tenants because I have had bad experiences with tenants who know the laws better than City Hall."

"Cocoa Panyol, I'm looking for a place for my brother. He lives by me; he's too friendly with my woman; and I don't trust him," Hamid said.

"Hamid's brother looks as a ready-made-trouble package. Don't you think so, Dunkirk?"

"Plenty trouble, Cocoa Panyol. By the way, you have a Trini accent."

"I've been in this country over fifty years, but I still keep that Trini accent, except I don't sing my words as most Trinis do. But I know when to switch to American conveniently."

"I just came from dancing in a Trini steelband in Baisley Pond Park. The Trinis were celebrating their fifty-seventh year of Independence from England."

"Who wants to be dropped first?" Hamid asked.

"Cocoa Panyol, would you mind if Hamid drops me at your address to see if your apartment will suit my taste?"

"Sure. But aren't you going back by your loving boyfriend to return his cargo pants and to dress up tonight in silk?"

She did not answer his question, but said, "Cocoa Panyol, can I come to see your apartment?" Her voice was commanding.

"It's dusty. But, surely, you can come and do the dusting."

"Janitors don't mess up the place because they know they will have to clean up the mess."

"Dunkirk, I've heard that line before. Please, don't use that overworked saying to bamboozle me."

"Cocoa Panyol, did you hear friendship is not whom you have known longest. It is who walked into your life, said, 'I'm here for you,' and proved it. Cocoa Panyol, you have proved your friendship in less than half an hour. I hope we remain friends, and one day I can return your kindness." She stretched her hand; and he shook it firmly.

Dunkirk's sadness left her. She knew she could not go back by Darwin because if he would take her in, Eldika would not, because Eldika knew she left to meet Jason at the airport. Worse still, Eldika believes her father loves Dixie, but Dixie used him.

In a happy tone, she bounced his knee, and said, "Who gave you the nickname, Cocoa Panyol?"

"My father before he died. He was a farmer who planted cocoa in his large estate. He picked me up at Forest Reserve E.C. School in Trinidad and called me so, and the school children never forgot it. I can recommend a book that speaks of Cocoa Panyol Language and Culture by Dr. Satnarine Balkaransigh, Dr. Patricia E.D. Belcon, and other Trinidad and Tobago scholars. The name of the book is *Re-Igniting The Ancestral Fires: Heritage, Traditions, And Legacies of the First Peoples.*"

"Where can I get a copy of that history

book to buy?"

"I have an extra copy. That book speaks of the history and culture of Trinidad and Tobago people."

"How much for that book?"

"It is my gift to you, if you read and discuss the book with me. I study that book as my catechism, and I 'drink deep' of the copious knowledge that book imparts."

Hamid stopped at Cocoa Panyol's address on Greene Avenue, Brooklyn, and Dixie stretched her hand to tip him. Cocoa Panyol blocked her hand, and handed Hamid the fee and a sizable tip.

She stretched as she came out of the car, did a bending exercise that she usually does whenever she enters Baisley Pond Park, and she kept talking. "Does that mean you'll really rent me, a nobody, in cargo pants and a dirty, smelly top, an apartment in your beautiful brownstone?"

"Yes; but you have to read that book from cover to cover and discuss it with me." He entered the building through the basement door.

"By your age without the bucket hat (both laughed), I gather you are retired; you have acquired some wealth; you have this three-story brownstone with a furnished basement without tenants; and reading is your hobby. I have a long time before I get my social security. I will only have time to read sometimes after work."

"I'm going to prepare dinner for us. There are three apartments above this basement. Each apartment has a bathroom with a shower and a tub. There are clean towels in closets on each floor. In the drawers are pajamas, nighties, and dresses that my wife had never worn. She was a shopaholic. All styles are there, name them. Choose whom you wish. You will find enough clothes of your cute size to dress and go and shop in Manhattan tomorrow."

"I have my Citi debit card and cash in my cargo pants. I'd probably need a loan, but not right now. Cocoa Panyol, what's your Christian name?"

"I have so many bloods in me; I don't know if I'm Christian."

"What name is on your driver's license?"

"John Pitkins, my dear."

"John Pitkins, were it not for your kindness, tonight I would have been homeless for the second time in my life. I prefer to call you Cocoa Panyol."

"When my schoolmates meet me in Brooklyn that's how they greet me."

"When I didn't call you Cocoa Panyol or C.P., you should know I'm angry with you."

"For now save your anger, Dix. Go upstairs. When you come back, dinner will be served, and we can talk without sleeping tonight. Today is Saturday so you can go and shop at Macy's, or wherever you choose to shop tomorrow to get clothes for your job on Monday."

She went upstairs and showered almost an hour. She returned in a new robe with Pamela Roland tag and soft slipper, all made for her size. Her hair was short, black, and curly.

"How do I look, C.P.?"

"More beautiful than my two beautiful daughters, just blacker, and I love black women."

"What about your wife? Was she black

too—her color, I mean, not her race, because, I'm sure, race was no problem with handsome and muscular you?"

"Laundry is the only thing that should be shared by color. I set the table, so let's eat."

"You cooked all this food while I was in the shower? And your food is presented as an abstract art."

"Yes, I cooked while you were in the shower."

"Does that mean I spend too much time in the shower that I will have to share the water bill with you? My boyfriend used to be annoyed when I stayed long in the shower."

He smiled.

"You never asked for my story, and how I got into this predicament. But I will tell you."

"How do you like my cooking, Dix?"

"It's soooo goood. I'll buy you aprons for our anniversary."

"What anniversary would that be?"

"The Cocoa-Panyol-Good-Samaritan Anniversary with Dix." She didn't let him ask another question because she wanted to talk of her life. "The man who loves me dearly, and we were about to get married, I walked out of his house as an ungrateful bitch. I left his house to meet the man I truly love. I was hoping to meet him at J.F.K. because he was taking me to Florida to live with him. He left his job at a Fortune 500 company in New York to assume a job as a consultant in Florida at Power and Light."

"What's his name?"

"Jason."

"Didn't Jason know you were coming?"

"No. He had been asking me for many weeks to come; he had bought two Delta airline tickets for us to travel together; and I never gave him an answer. But this morning I rushed out to meet him and lost the flight. Then found myself homeless for the second time."

"Why not go back to the man you were going to marry? He'll rush to marry before you change your mind again."

"If we are lovers—and I know that will never happen—and I'd done to you what I did to that man, would you have welcomed me back with opened arms?" She looked him in his eyes. "Speak the truth, Cocoa Panyol."

"I wouldn't marry you. But I had a similar situation—worse than yours."

"I don't want to hear it. Would you mind if I cook your dinner tomorrow?"

"Only if you discuss the Balkaransingh-Belcon book tomorrow. That book is one of the best books I've read. To me, it is as good as Eric Williams' *Capitalism and Slavery*. Eric Williams was one of the foremost research scholars in the world. Read my book and compare it with Williams'."

"Not this week. I have to go shopping for clothes and my workload is heavy. I am the editor of a newspaper, and I also research for a nonprofit organization. I studied one thing in college, and I'm doing something else to get money."

"I did many odd jobs as a new immigrant to keep my survival afloat. I cleaned warehouses at nights till mornings, and went straight to my day job after showering in the different warehouses."

"But that was not your main job?"

"It was not. I was a troubleman at a bank."

"The man I was going to marry was also a troubleman at a bank. He told me he corrected all the items in difficulty, and he spoke to the traders." She smiled when she said, "Cocoa Panyol, you are around since Allan Greenspan was Chair of the Federal Reserve. That means you are seventy or seventy plus?"

"Seventy."

"You are like good wine?"

"And good wine needs no bush."

"How many women of varied races drank the good wine from your cup?"

"You are too under-aged to know."

"Am I unsafe under your roof?"

"In what way?"

"If I'm in a dark room discussing the book, and I bring wine in your class...."

"You just said your workload on your job is hectic and you are tired."

"Soon, I'll be able to."

"How come?"

"I'm going to stop working overtime. Too many people have to do overtime because they buy-and-buy nonstop and run up their credit cards that they will never finish paying after retirement. I am not one of those shopaholics."

"Dix my dear, you had a long day. Go to sleep. All your rentals are paid in advance by Cocoa Panyol who came from a place that had the First Peoples that Columbus met. He didn't discover us."

"You have that fiduciary responsibility for me?"

He smiled.

She went to bed and slept like an angel without fears. She awoke and put herself in the clean tub. She filled the tub with hot water and realized the water was too hot for her body. She let hot water run out, and when the tub was half full, she turned on cold water till the water in the tub was comfortable for her bath. She rested her head on the wall and felt the world is once again kind to her. "Lord, who am I?" She wrapped herself in a towel as she stepped out of the tub and asked the Lord another question. "Lord, am I lost?"

There was a knocking on the door. "Dix, Cocoa Panyol made breakfast. Don't let your coffee get cold."

"I'll be down in ten minutes."

It was November but she was dressed in the house as if she were in the Arctic zone. She sat at the table and waited on the host.

"Good morning, Dix. How was your sleep?"

"That bed is so comfortable; the sheets are spotless. A professional designer decorated that room for the Duchess of Sussex?"

"I notice you make mention of her quite often. You like her?"

"Very much but the English press is saying uncharitable things about her and her child."

"Does that surprise you?"

"Not really."

"I hope you like my breakfast, and you will not do as the Panyols in my T&T country that I left to migrate to here."

"What they do?"

"My mother told me after Panyols eat, they wipe their mouths and leave because if they remain, they will tell lies."

She laughed nonstop. Then she was cerebral in her thinking. "I can't wipe my mouth and leave. I have no place to go."

"You can go to another apartment upstairs or come to the basement."

"Rental near the landlord downstairs may be too expensive."

"You can barter."

"What for what?"

"You do the cooking; I do the cleaning."

"The two-way helper you told me about will not be coming again to clean?"

"No."

"She left or you fired her?"

"It was a civil ending."

"Have you more scrambled eggs left in the pot?"

"No; but I can quickly scramble two for you."

"Scramble it for the two-way helper. She may drop by to ask back for her job."

"She left with a huff and a puff."

"I haven't heard that line since I left kindergarten."

He looked at her. "You used to huff and puff at your teacher when you were in kindergarten, and she told you to sit and stop talking?"

She laughed. "You can hire me. But you will have only one-way service from me!"

He laughed and laughed.

"What's so funny, C.P.?"

"My house is always warm. Why do you cover yourself as if you are going to shovel snow? Even if you are naked, I will not look at you or attempt to touch you."

"You never had a woman since your wife died?"

"Yes and no."

"Which is it—yes or no?"

"More no than yes."

"C.P., I wish you revert to only yes. The female body is God given."
'Yours?"

"Of course. Haven't you noticed when I had loose clothes on? Are you gay or both ways?"

"You'll have to find out."

She knew he was lying. She told herself if he were not straight, he wouldn't care if she were covered in winter clothes from head to foot. Driving home in Uber she could feel his sexual temperature whenever her leg carelessly touched his. She felt the same way too, and she would be jubilating in her mind, rejoicing, and wishing for the day to come of what is in her mind to be true. She also saw the way he

looked at a woman with half of her breasts that hanged like low fruits, and when she looked at his eyes she saw he wanted to pick them. When Cocoa Panyol looked at the woman, she was reminded of the day she met Darwin in Baisley Pond Park. While Darwin talked to her in the park he looked at female joggers, especially those with moving derrieres in panty-sized shorts, and his eyes almost dropped out.
Cocoa Panyol read her thoughts and asked, "About what are you thinking?"

"The two men who are no longer in my life: One, I chose the shadow in the water rather than the bone in my mouth; the other, my stupid indecision ruled my life."

She picked up the dirty dishes and was putting them in the washing machine.

He said softly, and touched her shoulder, "Dix, that's not the dishwasher."

"Sorry. I'm not thinking right these last six months since I'm here."

"Dix, Dix, please, live in the present; those two men are gone." He took the dishes from her hands; she cried aloud; he led her to the couch; and he let her continue to cry aloud. When she wouldn't stop, he went on the couch, hugged her, and she rested her head on his shoulder. “Dix, as I grew older, I’ve come to the conclusion that love is like present-day politics; we have to do a lot of repositioning to win else we remain in the same gutter. Dix, just remember people who beat a dog, have to wait for the dog’s master.”

Crying a little softer, she said, “What do you mean? And call me Dix for the rest of our lives because I always wanted to be called with one syllable.”

“Dix, put your mind on someone else. Forget those two men.”

“Who?”

“A future man.”

Her crying ceased, and he removed his embrace.

“Cocoa Panyol, embrace me, embrace me. Don’t remove your hands from me, not so soon.” He obeyed.

Both were silent for a while.

“Dix, let’s go to a movie.”

“Not a love movie!”

"See, we have similar likes and dislikes. Both of us hate love movies. It ends the same way—man gets woman, woman gets man; and they go to bed after arguing about nothing. Sometimes they purposely fight because sex is better after a fight."

"I'm going upstairs to finish my thoughts in the tub. You had been interrupting me every day to come for breakfast, lunch, and dinner for all those six plus months I have been living in your brownstone. When I'm finished, come and massage my aching back, please."

"I did breakfast, lunch, and dinner for six plus months and I was not compensated; I dried your tears many days, plus today, neither was I compensated any time. How would the masseur be compensated?" Both laughed.

"In cash or in kind, Cocoa Panyol?"

"You pay for the movie. I'm seventy plus soon; and I don't know your bargaining tricks as other industrious women's so I want the money in my hand before we leave the house, not a promissory note."

It was the first time her smile was that broad. She walked upstairs flossing to Cardi B's *Press, Press, Press, Press, Press, Cardi don't need more press.*

Cocoa Panyol put the dirty dishes in the dishwasher, swept the kitchen floor, and said, "Alexa, shuffle Miles Davis." Alexa answered, "Shuffling Miles Davis on Amazon music." He raised the volume as Miles Davis' muted trumpet played *Blue in Green.*

Dixie shouted from upstairs, "That's the right music for my massage, C.P. Wash your hands and come right away."

He rushed upstairs and knocked.

"Come in masseur. I hope you washed the detergent off your hands for twenty seconds before you touch my sensitive, black, bounteous body."

"Dix, I want to keep this moonlighting job so I will obey all your rules now and in the future."

"I hope so." She was lying on her stomach, naked.

His navel an inch from her face, said, "Tell me when to begin, Dix."

"I love my minute name so much. I will shorten your name too. Begin, Panyol. When you put me out, I will write you love letters signed: Your Dix Forever. And I know you will be sorry for letting go this black BB."

"What BB stands for—not black bitch, I hope?

"BB stands for bounteous beauty."

"You prefer me with heavy hands or soft hands on your back?"

"Does that mean you are only going to massage my back before we go to see a love movie?"

"I thought you hate love movies."

"Your Panyol touch makes me change my mind. I think I'll ask the Peyai, the traditional healer in the land of the humming birds if we will be compatible in our behaviors if we get married."

"You are a lying, son of a bounteous, beautiful bitch! You read *Re-Igniting The Ancestral Fires* and pretended you never heard of that book. I will never trust you and what you know about life, mine, especially."

"I know Dr. Patricia E.D. Belcon. She calls herself 'a Socio-Carnivalist.' I went to the launching of that book in Medgar Evers College. I read it from cover to cover in one night."

He took his hands off her; she got off the padded table, threw a large towel over her body to cover her nakedness, and said, "Is there gayness in the Cocoa Panyol Culture?"

He pulled the towel forcefully off her. "You tell me." Before she said another word, his masculinity was on fire. His teeth were biting her firm breasts as if they were steaks, and they were waiting to be bitten. He lifted her, dropped her on the bed, and she did not move. He undressed quicker than flashed lightning and there he was, doing what craving men do; but she too was a craving woman, jubilating, singing, speaking love gibberish on the satin sheets on the queen-sized bed. She gasped, loudly. At seventy one, he was a man of the world—once a promiscuous man, married twice, missed marrying a third time, had overseas women whom he visited, in Barbados, in the Philippines, in Trinidad and Tobago, in France, in South Africa, and in Mozambique. Once he spoke French in her presence; this time he was making love like the Frenchman, foreplay first, orally, and said, looking in her eyes, "We are to own our own mistakes as our own, and our seeing daylight as our own."

"Please, Panyol, I'm ready."

"Not yet."

"When?"

"When you say you'll forget all your men of the past."

"Panyol, I forgot the past from the time you embraced me this morning. I felt your genuine care for me. I forgot those two men I told you about."

"Now you'll have it."

Their loving making was delicious. From the satin sheets off their bodies, they went in the full tub, made their own movie, came out, and he went on her bed again to relax.

She pulled him. "I need more."

"The gay Panyol wants to sleep."

"You are Caribbean, and you did not fool me."

"Add to that, Caribbean men get weary after sex too."

"If I'm lucky, I'll go through the years with you."

"Dix, your luck will never run out with me."

"That's a bet?"

"That's a bet."

"In blood and tears?

"In blood and tears."

"Goodnight."

"Goodnight."

CHAPTER 7

"Girls, I now have a three-letter name with one syllable."

"What Darwin calls you now?" Marce asked.

"He's out of my life."

"Dixie Dunkirk, what Jason calls you?" Marjorie asked.

"He, too, is out of my life."

"Who is this new Romeo who calls you by three letters," Jennifer asked.

"John Pitkins."

"What he calls you?" Marce shouted.

"Dix."

"Is he a musician who improvises when playing riffs, Dix?"

"He makes sweet music below my belly button."

"Miss Dix, lend him to me sometimes," Marce said.

Jill joined the women and men at the water cooler and asked, "What is it Marce wants to borrow from you, Dixie Dunkirk?"

"My man."

"Darwin or Jason?"

"They are past tenses."

"I know you were living with Darwin, and I'm sure he played good music below. What about Jason?"

"He never played there, Jill."

"How come?"

"He got a new job, and he didn't take me to Florida with him."

"What he does?"

"He is a CPM."

"What is that?"

"A cunt and prick man."

There was great laughter.

"Other than that, what Jason does?"

"He is an engineering consultant. He manages all the facets of a project to completion within budget in a given timeline."

"Jason is a bigshot, and you let him get away," Marjorie looked at Dixie.

"And he makes money moonlighting as a comedian."

"Have you ever gone to hear him on stage as a comedian?"

"Yes, at Comedy Central, Marjorie."

"How long is this very new Romeo in your bed, girl?"

"I'm in his bed."

"In a dirty railroad apartment?"

"In a three-story brownstone without tenants, and he lives in a beautifully furnished basement."

"He's a good soloist below?"

"Marjorie, he's an orchestra."

"Wow!"

"Dix, can I borrow your orchestra sometimes," Jill asked."

"His organ is too big for your studio."

"In what other ways you like your new Romeo," Agnes asked.

"He stopped buying me what I never had, and he has begun teaching me what I never knew."

"Only old people behave and make such comparisons. How old is he?"

"Seventy, seventy one, Jill."

"And you?"

"Forty, soon I'll be forty one."

"Soon you'll be the benefactor inheriting

the old man's brownstone and the legit owner of his bank accounts too. Be all in or all out, girl."

"That's what Aunt Ruby told Jason and me: There's no half way in life."

"You grew up with Jason?"

"Yes, Jonathan."

"And you wanted your little brother to fuck you?"

"He's not my brother, Jonathan; we just grew up in the same house."

"How come?"

"That's a long, long story; and it's not your fuckin business. Let's get back to work, guys."

Dixie Dunkirk is the editor of Real New York News, a newspaper with a two million circulation based in East 26th Street, Flatbush, Brooklyn. Although she and her staff are vulgar with their free speech, nevertheless, they know when it comes to their duties, her motto is: "Do it right the first time because I do not want Real New York News to be called fake news by the Trumpian Ambassador, the Unitary King, the

Radical in Chief, Individual 1, who told brown and black people—even though those brown and black people who are American Congresswomen—to go back to their infested country where you came from."

She continued: "Today, your task is to discuss which subject would be our headline tomorrow. Remember the head of the Trumpian Gang knows two words, one an adjective, the other and abstract noun—fake news. The Trumpian King is astute in retail politics, and his sheep are loyal to him as tight braziers that fit ridiculously painful on big breasts. His sheep's braziers stretch because the elastic they have to support their breasts become too weak to support the weight they carry; nevertheless, when the elastic bursts and the sheep's breasts fall out, the Trumpian King blames the breasts for getting bigger and not the his sheep's stupidity for buying a small brazier. And that's the Trumpian Way, and his policy to make America great again, forgetting America was always great, and his joy is to un-Obama everything President Obama legislated for the benefit of all Americans. His Republican buddies remain supine seeing and knowing his dishonesty in the extreme.

"Now let me hear your suggestions for tomorrow's headline. Please, be objective in your final choice regardless of your party affiliation."

There were countless shouts: RUSSIANS WERE IN THE WHITE HOUSE BY THEMSELVES WITH THEIR CAMERAS... THE TRUMPIAN KING SHUTS DOWN GOVERNMENT AND PUT 80,000 AMERICANS OUT OF A JOB...THE TRUMPIAN KING DECLARES NATIONAL EMERGENCY TO BUILD A BORDER WALL TO BLOCK OFF MEXICO AND ITS BROWN PEOPLE...GOD WANTED THE TRUMPIAN KING TO BECOME PRESIDENT AND GOD MADE HIS FIRST MISTAKE...WHEN THE TRUMPIAN VICE PRESIDENT CALLED THE TRUMPIAN KING'S NAME IN EUROPE EXPECTING WILD APPLAUSE, ALL THE EUROPIANS SAT ON THEIR HANDS...IN LESS THAN THREE YEARS THE TRUMPIAN KING TOLD MORE THAN 20,000 LIES...TWO BILLIONAIRES WANT TO BECOME PRESIDENT OF THE UNITED STATES.

"By the way, DO YOU BELIEVE THE PERFORMANCE OF COLTON UNDERWOOD, THE ADULT-MALE VIRGIN, AND CASSIE RUDOLPH OF THE BACHELOR SHOW ON ABC?"

"Dixie, I want to say something about the adult-male virgin who jumped over a high wall because Cassie told him that she didn't care for him."

"Go-ahead, Sara."

"Guys want what they can't have. When I told a dude I don't want him, he did the same to get out of my yard. In the past I was not able to hold my own in a relationship, and I let the man tell me his bullshit, and I ate it."

"What you do differently now to stop eating a man's bullshit? But from what I heard, you are still eating a little shit, Sara," Ampora said.

"I, too, heard you still eat a little, Sara," Azora repeated.

"I am not you, Azora!" Sara said.

"Sara, I was born in Brooklyn, not in Pakistan. From day one, I never showed any man I'm desperate. If I want to be laid, I want it in my house; if he's good, I will let him sleepover; if he's not good, even if it is raining, I show him the door. No man can use me as a forever-running Duracell battery." Azora smiled.

"With all your morality talk, I heard you always give it up on the first date, Azora."

"That's true—always to my dildo."

Everyone around the water cooler laughed, and she continued.

"Men love bitches; and I'm a senior bitch woman, because I tell men in advance who I am. I told a boaster who wanted to come between my sheets because he gave me some cash, let's have a conversation and see if you'll turn me on, and he backed out. He boasted so much of his virility. A real dick rises to the occasion always. I am not the nice woman who would drive from Brooklyn to Connecticut to get laid and leave. Me, this Brooklyn bitch, would not ask for money. I would give him five bills to pay from his debit card, and before I return to Brooklyn I must have the payment receipts on my iPhone."

Sara shouted, "Azora, you're a thieving ho!"

"Am a smart ho; am not like you, nice girl, who gives cheap or free pussy. I went to school; I know my values, and when I retire social security will be waiting on me. I know economics too. I am selective about my availability because I have to cover many grounds before sunset ends which is the wisdom of smart bitches."

"Azora, I never knew you moonlighted after work," Dixie said.

"Dixie, I never knew you dropped two young men and picked up an old man. Whenever I ask you what's the old man's age, you have been saying seventy plus for the past many years; by now he's seventy nine years plus three hundred and sixty four days."

There was laughter galore.

"Azora, the seventy-plus-old man speaks French when he's making love to me; I live free in his brownstone; he doesn't take a penny from me; and what is so nice I don't have to moonlight before sunset ends because that old man has energy to keep me in bed from sunset until daylight."

"Dixie, take my two-week's salary and lend him to me for a night."

"Your starving body hardly gets nourishment because you are saving your money to go back home. And, lest I forget, I never asked you which party you voted for, but I discussed my staff with Cocoa Panyol."

"Who's Cocoa Panyol," Lumkam asked.

"The old man I'm in love with. He told me to tell you all to read *Re-Igniting The Ancestral*

Fires: Heritage, Traditions, And Legacies of the First Peoples of his country, The Republic of Trinidad and Tobago, and compare it with the First People of America."

Dahoot stood as if he's defending himself in court. "Dixie, you said you only want to hear objective findings, but my subjective finding is...."

"Stop there, Dahoot."

"If I can't express an opposing thought of who are the First People in this country, I will leave."

"The door is wide opened for those who wish to leave and to those who prefer to have their headline ready for tomorrow. Good night. See you tomorrow." She kissed Dahoot before she walked out, spoke in her ear, and said, "Danny Boy, you come from a different continent and we are both black. We swim in the same pond, and the powers-that-be see us as un-American." She drove off in the beautiful Buick Cocoa Panyol bought for her.

As Dixie opened the gate to the brownstone, she was stopped by a businessman. "My name is Harry Z. Helmut. By the way you are professionally dressed I know you own this brownstone. I'll give you two million cash. No middleman will be in your business."

"My husband is more reasonable than I. He'll take forty million from you. What do you say, Helmut Zee?"

"Let me think."

"Helmut Zee while you are thinking, think of going home to jump on your fat wife's belly, and she'll tell you that you are not doing it right because your dick is soft and the ceiling needs painting. Right?"

He rushed out the gate and sped off in his Ford.

She rushed downstairs laughing aloud. "Cocoa Panyol, a man named Helmut Zee came to purchase your brownstone."

"Dix, how much he offered?"

"I told him you'll give him black, beautiful and bounteous Dix instead of the house at any price."

"Not the Dix who believes the only way to get rid of the temptation of falling in love with the seventy-plus-old man is to yield to him."

"You are plagiarizing Oscar Wilde."

"I'm reading what other lovers say to keep me updated when in love with a younger woman."

"One of my staff members told me older men love young women."

"His reason?"

"It was Penny."

"The pretty Jewish-Russian woman?"

"Yes, she."
"I cooked what you like."

"Penny says her husband is old, too, and he cooks whatever she likes."

"You and Penny discussed the *pros* and *cons* of falling in love with an old man?" She did not answer. "How old is Penny's husband?"

"I never asked her."

"How old is Penny?"

"My age."

"You never told me your age."

"I told you when your excess weight was on my belly last night."

"I forgot. Let's eat, my beautiful, bounteous, black woman. Tonight you'll be on the old man's belly, flyweight, and I'll be looking to see if the ceiling needs painting." The phone rang, and thinking it was a business call, he pressed speaker, French was spoken to him, and he answered, "Je vous aime, et vous aimeral toujours. Mon amour pour vous brille comme le soleil de midi, éclatant de beauté comme la lueur de la pleine lune dans la prairie isolée." The conversation ended with the caller.

"Cocoa Panyol, you are so fuckin disrespectful in my face. I will never let you get on my belly ever after telling that French ho, in front of my face, you love her, and you will always love her. And your love for her will always shine like the midday sun, and will be beautiful as the full moon in glow in the lonely meadow."

He looked at her, shocked. When he spoke French to friends on the phone before, she behaved as if she were ignorant of the French language.

"You can boast that you are proud to be a

descendant of the original peoples of T&T, but, I, too, can boast that I am a college graduate; French was my favorite foreign language; and my grades in French were always A's."

"Dix, that's an old friend; and we always wax childishly poetic when greeting each other. That flame is long extinct. We are both senior citizens."

"Senior citizens who fuck whenever they meet, I'm sure. When next are you going to get French pussy?"

"Yours is what I long for. May I get some later tonight, my only love?"

"Not tonight! Last year you went to France. Did you stay by her or in a hotel?"

"I stayed by her for French fries only." His smiles dimpled.

"I don't care what you ate, but if you had lied, I was moving out tonight not having any place to go."

They looked at each other and burst out in laughter.

"Dix, may I pour you a glass of wine?"

She looked at him. "Thank you, my love."

"Dix, can I tell you why I learned French, and how many French women jilted me?"

"Panyol, you had French *tabanka* many times?"

"Who taught you that T&T slang, and *tabanka* means a jilted lover's grief?"

"Elias, who was born in T&T, but his parents are Syrians."

"You have a federation in your newspaper employ."

"And I practice speaking foreign languages with them, Cocoa Panyol. If ever I let you go on my belly again, only French to embark and Portuguese to disembark."

He sang, "Ah, Cherie, my love for you is tres, tres fort."

She sang, "Wish my French were good enough, I'd tell you so much more."

"Let's go in the tub and do it, darling, je vous aime beaucoup."

"Cocoa Panyol, I was waiting on your invitation to the tub to do it as the French woman I saw on Optimum On Demand when you were sleeping."

"What she did?"

"I'll show you."

Her clothes were off first, but his organ got excited before her clothes were off.

Their night was a lovely tune. And their lovemaking was part of their ecstatic culture.

At work early next morning, Dixie began the new day with these words: "We had a long discussion yesterday on what you will write on, and the paper I like best will be the headline for today. But today, in less than thirteen hours, thirty two people from El Paso, Texas, and Dayton, Ohio, were the victims of mass murders. In El Paso, twenty nine people were killed by a white nationalist who traveled over six hundred miles to come and murder Hispanic people in El Paso. He called them invaders because he heard his President of the United States call Hispanic immigrants INVADERS. One week later an adult choke-slammed a thirteen-year-old boy because the boy did not take off his hat when the national anthem was played. The choke-slammer's reason for his cruelty to that little boy is: "That's what the President would expect me to do." Dixie drank a bottle of water. She never took the bottle from her mouth, only when it was empty. "Who wishes to speak?" she asked.

"I."

"Go-ahead, Culpepper."

"The President—I prefer to call him Moscow Putin's buddy—is an immigrant extract. He forgot two of his three wives are immigrants, and his present wife's immigration status when she arrived in the United States remains a hard-to-believe-true-story. That wife's sister and parents are in the God-Bless-the-United-States by way of chain migration. And the Trumpian Master's grandfather came into this country without documents...."

Dolan shouted, "And he could not speak English. And in Florida, the Trumpian Pied Piper asked his flock, how do we stop these invaders from coming into our country, someone shouted with alacrity, "Shoot them!" and the President smiled pleasantly." Dolan sat down.

Cave Man stood. He got that nickname because he does not speak, and he only wears jeans. He only writes. The group's eyes were transfixed on him wondering what he'd say. He began: "Elizabeth Warren says convincingly Trump is a white supremacist. I will vote for her to become the President of the United States because she doesn't speak with water in her mouth. She never equivocates. The man running to be president, long before he became president, his macabre compulsion was to award the death penalty to four, innocent, black boys who were wrongly accused for the death of a woman in Central Park.

"The man who said he can shoot anybody on Fifth Avenue and nothing will happen to him, also said for more than five years Present Barack Obama is not an American, and he never apologized, having told over twenty thousand lies before his 320 days in the White House. He is the mouthpiece for white supremacist. In his lies, he said he hasn't a drop of a racist's blood, but he's doing nothing to stop what racists do. He calls the white supremacist in Charlottesville good people, and the white supremacist called Jews by derogatory names and told the Jews to the top of their voices YOU WILL NOT REPLACE US. Without shame, those white supremacists caused Heather Heyer's death. Individual One's supporters in Congress, Moscow Mitch, Doonbeg Pence, and Republican Senators of similar ilk are waiting on the TKL businessmen on TV who does odd jobs to weed out the injustices Individual One sows.

"George F. Will, noted journalist, says, Trump doesn't just pollute the social environment with hate. He is the environment. He is an entertainer, and an entertainer feeds on his audience."

Cave Man continues. "Some of the living victims who suffered from the white supremacist's bullets did not want the President to come to El Paso, and he should go to the graves of the dead Hispanic victims and apologize, posthumously, to them. The white supremacists are saying power is slipping away from them because of the influx of black, brown, Asian, and other immigrant people, and the way they, the white people, have been doing things is no longer the way things are done. In 2045 whites will be in the minority and feel they will be black and brown people's servants.

"Donald Trump's aim is to make America a white Christian country.

"He has carried on a grievous campaign of xenophobia, misogyny, racism, shrieking rallies, listening to his minions shouting 'shoot the invaders' and there he was smiling instead of telling them don't say that. It was sad. He has measured out what decency is—with lies and no compassion for the less fortunate.

"Trump's former White House Communications Director says his President incites hate and death threats; he will no longer support Trump's re-election because Trump is a pernicious evil; and let us throw water on the green witch.

"Casablanca is the movie that has everything for everybody, and I am going to see it to get rid of Trump fear. Good night."

He sat down, and he received a thunderous applause.

"Dixie, I'd like to talk about Trump's *quid pro quo*."

"Leave that for another day Culpepper."

As Dixie drove home thinking what would America become if Donald J. Trump becomes victorious in the year 2020, she sang *We shall overcome*, and tears dripped from her eyes.

CHAPTER 8

Her cell rang one minute after midnight. Dixie was wondering whom could it be. "Hello."

"Dixie Boom Boom!"

"Yes, Aunt Ruby! How are you?"

"Trouble! Trouble! Trouble!"

"Who is in trouble?"

"Poonks, Poonks!"

"What's wrong with Jason?"

"I remember when both of you were children, you had a blood test and it showed you have O-negative, that rare blood. Jason is badly damaged in a traffic accident, and his doctor says he needs O-negative blood. Would you help Poonks, Dixie Boom Boom?"

"Aunt Ruby, I will, with the last drop of blood in my body. I will sacrifice my life to save him. Every night I go to bed thinking of his words: Ask Aunt Ruby. She helps everybody."

"Jason, Uncle Roy, and I now live in Florida, and since Jason returned from New York he put my name as joint owner on his bank accounts, and for his age he has plenty money. I will be paying all your expenses for all the time you live in Florida with him before you go back to New York. I've bought you a one-way ticket. Can you leave today?"

"Today?"

"Yes; today."

"Sure."

"God will bless you, my child. It was a blessed day I took you and your mother in to live with us." She hung up.

"Dix, since you answered that phone, black you are red as blood."

"Panyol, I'm black times black; I'm not

half breed as you."

"I'm less than half breed: My mother told me she's mixed with black, Indian, Spanish, Carib, Syrian, and English, name it."

"What made your complexion change, so differently from your teenage picture on the wall?"

"I don't know. Probably I spend too much time in the sun."

"Cocoa Panyol, the little boy, now a man, who took me and my mother off the streets of Brooklyn and from sleeping in Marine Park, got in a serious car accident, and the doctor says he needs my O- negative blood to save his life."

"Can he not get it from a relative where he lives? Where does he live?"

"In Florida." She didn't delay with her next sentence. "And I am traveling today to give him blood."

"Dix, you can have my debit card and my pin number."

"Panyol, all my expenses are already paid up to the time I remain in Florida."

"Traveling, first class?"

"Yes."

"Hotel?"

"I will be in a house."

"Who is this little boy, now a man?"

"He is the man I was going to meet 1600 hours at JFK on the day we met in Uber."

"Have a safe trip, Dix. Those airlines give you a soda and a stale, baby pretzel for lunch." He smiled.

She didn't. "Aren't you going to question me?"

"About what?"

"If you are really in love with me you would ask, 'When am I returning? Who is this man? Are you or were you in love with him?'" He didn't answer. "Say something. Let one of your bloods—let the dominant, warlike, Carib blood in you say something if the English blood is too docile and diplomatic to speak."

"Next month June, I will be thirty years

your senior. I've divorced twice and almost got married two weeks before we drove together in Uber. You are going to repay someone who cast his bread on the water for you, and it is now your turn. You called his names in your sleep when you lost the plane. I heard you from downstairs."

"What names did I call?"

"Poonks, Poonks, Jason, Jason, I missed the flight. Forgive me."

She came off the chair and ran into his arms. Crying, she asked, "If Jason wants me to remain with him, what I should do, Cocoa Panyol?"

"Dix, sometimes you have to send yourself roses, and going to be with him you'll know if he's the rose you want to send to yourself. Forget about the going-to-heaven life when you die. Your happiness is right here on earth. You and Jason need each other. I'm nearer to the grave than you. If you come back to me, soon I may be an Alzheimer's disease patient, and you'll have me as your burden. My last wife died from Alzheimer's, and I saw the painful burden of her caregivers, especially Mrs. Haye."

"That French woman loves you for your humanity. Can I describe the New York landscape to you in French when you drive me to JFK?"

"You'll have to take Uber."

"Why?"

"I won't be able to drive back to Brooklyn."

"Why?"

"My tears will flood and block my vision."

"Before your tears flood over, can we go in the tub and hide our tears, Cocoa Panyol?"

He hesitated.

"Cocoa Panyol, I will cook; you will enjoy dinner; and you don't have to remain after dinner. You can do as the original Panyols: After my serving you dinner, you can wipe your mouth and leave, because if you remain you will tell lies to me. You will tell me in your old age you stop putting Frenchie to bed, and you don't have children born in France. I have to sleep on that one."

They were drying each other's body and still laughing aloud. Her eyes were brimming for she knew she may never return to his kindness once she sees Poonks who rendered yeoman's kindness to her and her mother, but Cocoa Panyol's kindness was magnanimous. She took him to sit in the loveseat, and they spoke of their past life. Daylight was quickly approaching when she'd leave him.

"Why are you crying, Dix, my love?"

"Because you may not be hugging me again, John Pitkins."

"Wherever you go, never stop calling me Cocoa Panyol."

"Not today. John Pitkins, tell me something about you that I don't know so if I never come back I will remember it."

"I invited a beautiful woman for dinner. She told me a habit she indulges in whenever someone invites her to dinner. I told her I hope she doesn't practice that habit around the dinner table again because once was enough."

She got up, and walked out.

"What was that bad habit, John Pitkins?"

"You never did it; neither would you do it."

"Please, tell me."

"All the dishes and cutlery were perfectly washed in the dishwasher and wiped dry by the helper. But she took the napkins on the table and wiped for more than five minutes every dish and cutlery on the table. I told her that her knowledge of etiquette is a minus, less than uneducated peasants' she so often criticized. She left the table, blazed me with obscenity, asked for her car fare. I called Uber, and she walked out and slammed the door."

"Many times, I say, 'Ole man, pass me this or that.' Is it bad table manners to call you ole man when we are dining?"

"I'm old."

"Do I do it better than Frenchie?"

He laughed endlessly.

"Let me ask you an easier question."

"I hope it is not about the French Revolution and Marie Antoinette telling the people to eat cake."

"No."

"Then, what is the non-French question?"

"What is the best day of your life?"

"Today."

"Because I'm leaving, and your brownstone will be a place where the two-way helper can return to do your bidding."

"Not that."

"Then what?"

"I see daylight, and I'm sure I'm alive. Life is the toughest school and I survive without cheating."

"I thought you would have said because I'm in your arms?"

"That too."

"What else? You can tell me a little of your life."

"I once lived opposite a landlord who had a dummy resembling a man holding on to the ledge of his building as if that man is in danger of falling, and the man needs someone to rescue him from falling. That landlord enjoyed seeing people standing in amazement, some calling the police to help the falling dummy. I had a woman whom I had loved dearly, and she was similar to that landlord."

"In what way, John?"

"She treated me as if I'm that dummy."

"Did you fall off her ledge?"

"Yes."

"Did I build you up and will be leaving you for Poonks at a moment's notice just as that woman whom you had loved, and who left you hanging on the ledge and let you fall not having her love?"

"Absolutely not! Let me put my analogy another way: Don't die with your dreams, accomplish them, risky and non-risky, vulgar and non-vulgar, so you can boast of them in your rocking chair when you are old."

"Poonks and I are now adults who have not been in touch for many years; our childish love can disappear in our adult life. What if we are not compatible in our way of life, and I return to the ole man?"

He smiled. "Who's that stupid ole man who makes bad choices—instead of having Frenchie in bed for his birthday tomorrow? He is sad to see his black beauty leaving Brooklyn for the sunshine state."

"I'm bleeding inside because I will not be there to celebrate your seventy third birthday."

"I am bleeding inside too. You brought me into your world, and I enjoyed every day from the day I stepped into Uber older than Methuselah with my sweaty hat and you in your cargo pants."

"Would you be thinking of me if I never return?"

"I don't know. I may have dementia."

"Before you get dementia, which you may never have, would you think of us in the tub together?"

"Not with the cold water you turned on purposely."

"The man I left did that to me."

"Why?"

"So that we will not stay long in the tub."

"Why he did that?"

"To cut his expensive water bills."

"That's one of the reasons why you left him?"

She did not answer.

"I read somewhere, Dix, people don't abandon people they love; they abandon people they were using."

"I wasn't using him. Jason invited me to come with him to Florida many months ago, and I didn't make up my mind to leave Darwin."

"What was preventing you from leaving Darwin?"

"We came to the point where we were just respectful of each other, but it was a comfortable life for both of us."

"Even in bed your respect for him overpowered your passion?"

"Yes, even in bed, Cocoa Panyol. Would you miss me when I'm gone later today?"

"Sure!"

"Next week?"

"Sure."

"If I have to stay with Jason until he gets better, and when he gets better, I want to come back to be with you, would you take me in?"

"That's not how life goes with old people, Dix."

"You tell me how life goes with old people."

"I, too, may be in need of help and cannot wait on you. As such, I'll employ a helper. The helper may be kind and attentive to me, and I'll want her to stay with me forever."

"John Pitkin a.k.a. Cocoa Panyol, nothing will happen to you to need a full-time helper."

"How do you know?"

"You told me you come from a long line of healthy descendants; your father was riding his motorbike at eighty five; you rode on the saddle at the back of his motor bike; and he died at ninety four."

"Dix, let us stop talking about death; let's

go to bed before daybreak."

"Can I come to sleep downstairs on your bed and in your arms for the last time before I leave?"

"Dix, my arms are opened now and will be opened for you always."

They enjoyed each other's body very much.

"Cocoa Panyol, I don't want to shower. I want to continue to talk and to feel what you left inside of me germinating. Now I want to tell you everything about my life."

"You don't have to."

"I want to because I've never met a man in my life that I want to trust, and I trust you to the end of my days."

"Why? Why?"

"I learned recently oysters were first served to prisoners, now it is served to Presidents; and red wine was served to peasants. But I didn't have to learn you are a good man. I see it daily that you are a kind man with a solid, ethical core and integrity unmatched. You took me in not knowing who I am. I'm sure you had seen on TV the woman begging, sitting by the roadside, and a Good Samaritan took her in, fed her, clothed her, financed her, and when that kind man was away for couple hours that woman, who was pretending to be a beggar, let her pack of criminal friends back in a truck and cleared the man's house of all his valuables. I could have been that kind of woman."

"Jason, your loving Poonks, is an engineer who has more green notes than I would ever have. He would not come in Bed Stuy, in this poor part of Brooklyn, in Greene Avenue, with a truck and pilfer my 1930's stuff with black dust and grime. I read up on him."

"You did?"

"Yes, I did."

"Why?"

"At seventy three, I still have a little sense before dementia steps in because I know how to get info from Google."

"You ever sneaked into my phone while I'm asleep, as some men do, to get information about me?"

"It is the first time I'm exceedingly annoyed in the two-plus great years since I've known you. I go covertly into your phone? Never!"

"Cocoa Panyol, I'm very sorry. That's not how I think of you; and I will never think of you, overtly or covertly, going into my cell for information. Forgive me, please, please. Now I'm sorry that I did not go and shower and let you rub the dirt off my black back. "

"Where and when did you accumulate that dirt? You are cleaner and clearer than Poland Spring water."

"You will forgive me?"

He hugged her, and said, "This Cocoa Panyol needs more forgiveness for the things he has done from birth to the time he met you and now."

"Like what?"

"If I begin to tell you all the wrong things I did in my life, you'll miss your flight; don't forget you missed your first flight to travel with Poonks."

"I don't mind missing this second flight to be here with you."

"Don't forget Aunt Ruby said, frantically, Poonks needs your O-negative blood to live."

"Please, don't let me feel sad and ungrateful."

He hugged her. "In less than four hours you have to be on that plane, so catch a little sleep, and probably when you are up a certain part of my body will rise."

"I know a woman's trick that can make it rise now."

"Make what rise? Stop doing that to me."

She put his organ that had already risen on the lower part of his body in its rightful place on her body.

When the unison of flesh on flesh ended, she said, "Panyol, you never said I love you in a long time. Could you say it now as if it is the best love you have given to everyone including Frenchie?"

"I love you, Dix, more than I'd admit."

"How soon you'd want me to return?"

"I cannot answer that question."

"Please, answer it."

"After you shower, I'll answer it."

"After I get rid of your unloaded impurities, you'd give me an answer."

"I never knew what causes creation is called unloaded impurities."

"I can give you the name millennials call it."

"How do you know the name that millennials call it?"

"Come to the tub with me again, and I'll tell you."

"I want to make a sumptuous breakfast for you instead."

"I hope it is not the last one."

"The ball is in your court."

She looked at him. "I hope what you did this morning makes me pregnant, so I'll have to return back soon before Aunt Ruby notices what your impurities did."

They enjoyed breakfast and fed each other. She was dressed beautifully.

"How do I look Cocoa Panyol?"

"As sweet as the succulent cocoa pods I used to suck in my grandfather's cocoa estate when I was a boy."

"How you got to the sweet pods?"

"I climb the cocoa tree, picked the cocoa off the tree, burst the cocoa, and suck the sweet pods that are inside the cocoa."

"I will return quicker than you think for my cocoa to get burst and the pods get sucked. And I may give my cocoa a new name according to how the picker does the picking and based on how the fruit is sucked."

"You are a good comedian as Poonks, but I am not taking you to the airport."

Why?"

"I told you before I wouldn't be able to look at you walking away not to see you again."

"Just think of my sweet cocoa pods that need to be sucked and book my return flight to suck them next week."

They hugged and laughed joyously. As she walked to Uber, he shouted, "Don't forget my ceiling may need painting, and you are the one to tell me while you are on your back looking up at the ceiling singing, rejoicing, jubilating about the love I'm giving you on the new satin sheets you bought."

"Let the French woman from Paris come and paint it before your dementia presents itself."

"To hell with that French broad and that bitch named dementia! I love you only till the day I die."

"Say it again."

"This seventy-three-year-old man loves you only, Dix and until I die."

"I left a letter hidden in my pillowcase that speaks of my love for the older man who no longer loves the French woman named Aime and the coterie of women as much as he loves Dix who makes you holler in bed. Listen to what I am saying before I board Uber."

"I'm already listening."

"If I'm lucky, I'll go through the years

with you no matter your physical condition, your mental condition, or your sexual condition. Goodbye."

Uber drove off.

She cried a river.

He went home and asked Alexa to play Michael Feinstein singing *Grateful*. He fell asleep thinking of her gratitude in loving him with all his misgivings.

CHAPTER 9

Aunt Ruby and Uncle Roy greeted Dixie at Tampa Airport; tears dripped from Aunt Ruby's eyes, and she said, "Dixie Boom Boom, God is good. He brought you here safely. I don't know if Poonks will live because he's badly damaged in a motor accident. A kid, without a driving license, broke the red light and hit Poonks's car flush on the driver's side. Poonks served in the Navy, and I'm taking you straight to the Veteran Hospital in Tampa to give Poonks your O-negative blood. The doctor says your blood may or may not save him. But God knows best."

"Aunt Ruby, Poonks will have my blood and whatever part of my body the doctor says he needs. Because of him, my life is not in vain; and because of you, my mother and I did not sleep one more night in Marine Park."

Uncle Roy drove them to James A. Haley Veterans' Hospital to The Michael Bilirakis DVA Spinal Cord Injury Center and parked. He is a little man with sinewy arms, a dry smile, and shows little emotions, but as he got out of the car he hugged Dixie, and said in her ear, "Dixie Boom Boom, God blessed the day Poonks spoke the words, 'Ask Aunt Ruby; she helps everybody.' Now you are helping Aunt Ruby because giving Poonks your blood is like giving it to her. She loves that boy as if he's her own body."

"Uncle Roy, some years ago I lost the plane to meet Poonks, but if I didn't catch the plane today, I would have been devastated." They were still hugged.

Ruby separated them. "Let's go, Dixie Boom Boom. Roy, stay in the waiting room." They walked to the doctor in charge of the operating room. Ruby said, "Doctor, you remember me." He bowed. "This is Dixie Waltz Dunkirk. She's the person who will be giving my nephew, Jason, her O-negative blood."

"Ruby, this is how far you can go. Leave your number at the front desk. We'll call you whenever we are finished with Miss Dunkirk. Jason will be spending a long time here after his procedure today."

Ruby hugged Dixie, and both cried.

"Let's go, Miss Dunkirk. Time is of the essence," the doctor said.

"Doctor, when he awakes, tell him I'm here," she said.

"After the operation, you will tell him yourself."

After five hours, Jason opened his eyes, he smiled gently, and he whispered, "Stinky Boom Boom, I'm alive, and I thank you."

"Don't try to speak. I know you are Stinky Poonks; I am Pee-ah-Bed Boom Boom." She kissed him. "See, you don't have to fight me for a kiss. I gave it to you voluntarily."

"You left out those three important words," he whispered.

"I love you. Stop talking."

He closed his eyes; the doctor walked her out of the room and said, "Miss Dunkirk, he'll be spending some time to heal. I heard you live in New York. Jason's aunt is a retired RN, but she is a senior person who would need help. Would you be going back to New York soon to assume your duties?"

"No, doctor."

"What do you do?"

"I'm the editor for a newspaper."

"What do you think of our President, the Radicalizer and Liar in Chief who promised to send sick children who need medical help back to their country to die? Equally vindictive, he held up the money for the Ukrainians who are fighting Russia until they give him dirt on a political rival who will be fighting him in the presidential election."

"When Jason gets his release from you, I'll tell you what I think of him."

"You think I'll delay Jason's recovery if I'm a Trumper or non Trumper?"

"No doctor; but Aunt Ruby told Jason and me from childhood, 'If speech is silver, silence is gold.'"

One month later Dixie was again at James A. Haley Veterans' Hospital, her smile broader than the English Channel, she held Jason's hand, and told him to get up from his wheelchair.

"I am not fully healed, and you are already bossing me around." His smile deepened, and she kissed him on his forehead.

"Poonks, Uncle Roy is here to take you home. Didn't you beg him not to tell Aunt Ruby when he caught you peeping at me when I was showering in the bathroom?"

"No! That is not true."

"Well, as soon as we get in the car, I will tell Aunt Ruby what you did."

"That's thirty plus years ago, and she'd know you lied."

"Aunt Ruby had been preaching to you every day that it is a sin when little boys peep at their sisters, and if they continue to do that they will get blind."

"I knew you when I was five years old; you are not my sister! And I am not blind because I didn't peep at you when you were showering, Miss Pee-ah-Bed."

Aunt Ruby walked in on them. "Poonks, you are going home today. Did you kiss Dixie Boom Boom, tell her thank you, and if she's not married, you'd marry her."

"No, Aunt Ruby. But I'll ask her when I'm fully recovered and can go back to work to have enough money to support her as if she's the Duchess of Sussex who doesn't need the Queen's pounds."

They laughed, Dixie laughed loudest, and Aunt Ruby spoke. "Poonks, when I asked her to come, it was one minute after midnight, and she came that same day; so you are a blessed soul. Step in this chair and let me push you to the car."

"No, Aunt Ruby. Let me push this sneaky man quickly out of here. I caught him admiring a beautiful white woman. Since school days he admired white girls more than black girls, and Cash Nixon was his favorite white girlfriend. He wrote poems about her and for her." As he stood, Dixie supported him to the back seat, and Uncle Roy drove them safely home.

Dixie took Jason to a comfortable arm chair, and Aunt Ruby said, "I am the registered nurse, but I no longer work as a nurse since my life and time are spent in my orange business. Dixie Boom Boom, is it too much if I ask you to take care of Poonks in my absence—bathe him, wash his hair, prepare his meals, go in the pool and swim alongside him, no jumping from the springboard, and don't let him rule you as when both of you were children. You don't have to bribe him because your O-negative-blood favor canceled his long-ago favor; both of you are on even keel with your God-given favors. So, Dixie Boom Boom, would you grant me those favors?"

"Sure, Aunt Ruby, with my heart and soul."

Jason spoke. "Aunt Ruby, I have rules too; and here are my rules to you, two women: I can wash myself without help, and when people from my job visit me, please, don't call me Poonks. For that matter, both of you, please, stop calling me by that stupid name. What the hell does that name mean?"

"Okay, Mr. Jason Litco. And I hope you will not peep at adult Miss Dixie Dunkirk again, so if Uncle Roy catches adult Jason, you will not have to beg him not to tell me, because her body is more curvy and feminine now. I notice you have been glancing at her pretty legs when she wears shorts."

The trio laughed heartily; and before Aunt Ruby left the room she told Dixie to always sit close to Jason as a safety measure.

Life in Aunt Ruby and Uncle Roy's home

in Citrus Springs, Florida, was wonderful. As Jason increased in health, it seemed as if Dixie and Jason were children again. They argued; they ate from each other's plate; they hugged; he played the piano, and they sang as a duet before they went in their separate bedrooms at nights. But Dixie who was the better pianist when they were children never played.

Now fit as a fiddle, Jason took Dixie to his job, and introduced her, first, as the woman he's going to marry, if she agrees, and, second, as Dixie Waltz Dunkirk, the black, bounteous, and beautiful woman from Brooklyn, New York.

"Jason, why won't she agree to marry you?" the CEO asked.

"She's from Brooklyn, New York, Bill; and Brooklyn women change their minds—as quickly as they say yes, they say no."

"Miss Dixie, is it true you are alike our President who says something now on a subject, and five minutes later, he says something differently on that same subject?"

"Bill, I am apolitical in the extreme."
Jason said, "Bill, can I use Dixie as my secretary? In New York, she's the editor of a news-

paper so making her my secretary is a sort of a demotion for her."

"She'd have to work for you and Danny."

"Why Danny?"

"His secretary is on maternity leave."

"Who is?"

"I believe Rona is on maternity leave because of you, Mr. Litco. I saw your car many times in dark spots parked with her in it. With Dixie's beauty, you won't let her leave for Brooklyn without marrying her?"

"Bill, Brooklyn's black women don't take shit, and you just wrongfully made me the object of your shit. Are you saying that to let Dixie know you are my boss, and I have to take all your shit to keep my job? Rona and I are friends from the first day I came on this job. She has engineering skills and loves speaking about civil engineering because her father was a civil engineer, and that is all we always spoke about. Except..." He paused. "You want to know the exception, Bill?"

Bill didn't answer.

Jason didn't say the exception in front of Dixie, but when she walked back to his desk with him, he told her Rona is pregnant for Bill.

Bill called out, "Jason, Dixie will be your secretary. But let me interview her before you leave for the church to get married."

"I thank you very much, Bill. You have been instrumental in my climb in this Fortune 500 company, and I'll remember to invite you to our wedding."

On their way home, Jason said, "Dixie, what did Aunt Ruby tell us about some humans when we were children?"

"She said when you mix cat shit and ice cream, only the cat shit remains the same; so you are telling me Bill is akin to the smell of cat shit?"

"He bred the fuckin woman, but he was doing his best for you to say good bye to me, and when you leave for Brooklyn he will be happy."

"May I ask you a question, Mr. Litco?"

"Sure."

"Rona is what?"

"What do you mean?"

"Race."

"If Bill and Rona are white, the baby will be white."

"Rona is brown."

"And you are brown, too."

"But her baby will not be mine. It will be the baby of a white man."

"I believe you because your babies will only come from white women."

"Dixie Dunkirk, fuck you! There's nothing wrong if I love a white woman; but Bill's child will be his, not be mine."

"Mr. Jason Litco, you don't have to bark at me. I was once in love with a white guy, and he was a gentleman. So we are on even keel again."

"I didn't tell you I slept with them."

"The CPM didn't?"

Jason laughed loudly as Dixie held his hand as they walked to the dinner table. Aunt Ruby wanted to know why he was so happy.

Jason said, "Aunt Ruby, guess what happened today when I took that Brooklyn broad to work with me?"

"You pee peed your underpants and hid it under the car seat as in the good old days."

"Not that! Make one more guess."

"You told Dixie to marry you, and you'll be hers forever and ever, and you'd stop dating the women you brought here many times."

"Aunt Ruby, what race?"

"All were beautiful, white women, Dixie." Aunt Ruby addressed Jason. "At your job, you told Bill you are in agreement with him to expand the business."

"Better than that!"

"Nothing could be better than that, Mr. Litco"

"Ms. Dunkirk will be Mr. Litco's secretary."

"Not true! Not true! Is that true, Dixie Boom Boom?"

"The boss, after he interviewed me, said the job is mine; but it is now I, the Brooklyn broad, to accept the job."

Aunt Ruby looked at her similar to the days when she, Aunt Ruby, enforced the house rules for Dixie to follow. "What's preventing you from accepting the job in that Fortune 500 Company?" She pulled her chair and faced Dixie.

"I didn't say I'm not accepting the job. All I'm saying is: I'll have to weigh the *pros* and *cons* before I take the job."

"Dixie, what are these *pros* and *cons*? Are they secrets? Are you in love with someone in New York?" She pulled her chair even closer to Dixie, and Dixie looked away. Jason tried to interrupt her. Aunt Ruby said, "Jason, don't you have manners?" She brought her chair a breath closer to Dixie's "Can't you see I'm speaking to someone, and it is not you, boy? What the hell is wrong with you today?" She looked into Dixie's pupils. "Is this a man about Harry Belafonte's age, more or less?"

"Something like that."

“I am a healthy octogenarian, and my granny used to say to me in my youth: It’s better to be an old man’s darling, than a young man’s slave. Is it that type of man?”

Dixie, from childhood, knew Aunt Ruby inside out—when she’s happy, when she’s sad, when she’s pissed, and she, Dixie, also knew at that very moment Aunt Ruby was pissed. Dixie was sure Aunt Ruby wanted to know the man’s exact age. “Aunt Ruby, when I was forty, he was seventy; and that’s three years ago when we first met. We met when I missed the flight to meet Jason, and Jason didn’t wait for me; otherwise I would not have met that man to enjoy his kindness. His name is John Pitkins, but his parents’ pet name for him is Cocoa Panyol; he told me to call him Cocoa Panyol, because his name has historical connotation, and that makes him feel special when he reads of his name in a history book by Trinidad and Tobago scholars. The name of the book is *Re-Igniting The Ancestral Fires: Heritage, Traditions, and Legacies of The First Peoples.*”

Aunt Ruby’s inquisitive mind would have asked countless questions—‘What kind of name is that? What kind of book will have history about such a name? What parent will give her child such a blasted, stupid name?’ But she saw the annoyance of her impertinent attitude on Dixie's face, and she changed the conversation to something familial. "Dixie Boom Boom, the weekend starts tomorrow, so what about visiting my orange estate in Fort Meade."

"That's great, Aunt Ruby."

"I bought two new bathing suits for you. Put on the one that will fit tightly to show your cute body, and let's see who can stay under water in the pool longer. Jason is not in the competition because he is a fish."

Aunt Ruby is not only a registered nurse, businesswoman, and keen observer of life's travails, she's also the family sociologist and street psychologist, not by book learning or trade, but by the life and experience she gained in Brooklyn when she lived in a racially-charged neighborhood. When she questioned Dixie about who is her present lover, she was thinking of a number of ways to reconnect Jason and Dixie, romantically, even if they lived in different states. Aunt Ruby's secret was her fading health, and Jason is the only person she'd pass on her wealth to; and the only woman she'd want Jason to marry to inherit her wealth is Dixie. She ended questioning Dixie and handed her the tight-fitting-bikini-bathing suit.

When Jason and Dixie got out of the pool,

Dixie dried his body, brought his clothes which she chose for him, dressed him, and she also brought a cup of hot tea for him. Aunt Ruby observed all the other loving gestures Dixie made towards Jason: She cooked whatever Jason wanted to eat; she gave him his meds every morning; and when the trio was together, Dixie spoke in Jason's ear. Both knowing, from childhood, Aunt Ruby hated when they spoke Ebonics or bad grammar, and they purposely did that:

"Jason."

"Yes, Dixie Boom Boom."

"Am is going to divide the money Aunt Ruby give me to share between you and I."

They looked at Aunt Ruby's forehead that moved up and down, and continued with their bad grammar.

"Dixie Boom Boom."

"Yes, Poonks."

"I just received new news from my friend who lives in Australia about the fire there."

"Where is she at?"

"I think she's somewhere at."

They had a towel around Aunt Ruby's eyes and said, "Aunt Ruby, we blocked your eyes so you couldn't hear our conversation."

She replied, "You stupit chil-ren, I hear with my ears, not with my eyes. I heard your bad grammar, still your grammar was not as bad as our President's with his green verbs." All burst out in laughter.

Life in Aunt Ruby's Citrus Springs's home was a beautiful place that Dixie enjoyed until she stopped hearing from Cocoa Panyol. She called him many times and could not get him. When she finally got him, she asked, "My love, where have you been? I've called you many times and could not get you. Where the hell have you been, Cocoa Panyol?"

"I'd lost my cell," he said.

"The house phone, too?"

He didn't answer.

"Where are you now?"

"In France."

"Have you read my letter that I hid in my pillowcase?"

He did not answer.

"Slut, you've gone back to France to fuck that ho!"

"Dix, calm down. That's not why I'm in France."

"You hadn't time to read my love letter, but you have time to go to sleep in that stinking, ho's bed."

"Dix, Dix, listen to me."

"I'm mailing back your fuckin keys. You're so fuckin old. And you look older than Methuselah even without wearing your dirty bucket hat. I will remain with the young man to fuck me good. I always wanted his young dick in me to bring back sweet memories. Stay with your stinking, French ho!" She slammed her cell on the floor.

That day and night she was silent. She stayed in her room, worse still, she didn't sit by the table for dinner. When she came out of the room she said,

"Jason, I'm not taking the job."

He was just as calm, "Okay, Dixie Dunkirk."

He went and sat at the pool and played music.

Aunt Ruby was not calm. "Dixie, I overheard your conversation with that old man. Here's your cell. Uncle Roy put the pieces together. I don't know why he did that. When are you leaving to go back to that old man?"

"After I visit your Fort Meade orange estate."

"You don't have to force yourself to go there with me."

"Aunt Ruby, I'm not forcing myself. I want to go there where you and I will be alone."

"Is tomorrow fine?"

"Yes."

She went back in the bedroom and locked the door, but she could hear clearly the music coming from the direction of the pool. The voice was Tony Bennett singing *Young and Foolish* composed by Albert Hague. She began to cry, but when she heard the words, smiling in the sunlight, laughing in the rain, I wish that we were young and foolish again, she screamed.

Aunt Ruby burst her door opened, and shouted, "Dixie, why are you crying? What's wrong with you? "

"I don't know."

Aunt Ruby spoke to her nonstop. "You are no longer a child, Dixie Boom Boom. You are a woman. We are both women. You are in love with Cocoa Panyol, but you feel you should be committed to Jason by repaying your debt of kindness to him. You already repaid your debt handsomely. You gave Jason your sacred blood to save his life. Consider yourself free. When I was an RN and took care of a man many years ago, he thought he was going to die, and he told me a bit of his life. Would you like to hear it?"

"No, Aunt Ruby."

"You can compare what I'm going to tell you with your love life."

"Aunt Ruby, not tonight. I want to spend tonight with Poonks. I want to relive our childhood and tell him how much I love him. I bought a gift for him that I've been cherishing for years. On the back of that gift I've written,

Poonks, if ever you have to say dust to dust, ashes to ashes for me, please, let this gift be dropped in my grave on my casket, because even in death I will love you."

"This is a dark tale, Dixie, but go-ahead and tell me about the gift."

"The gift is a poem that Poonks wrote for me when he was seven years old. I'm returning it to him, embossed, and in a golden frame."

"You have that poem. My god! I thought I was the hoarder, but you beat me by miles. Can I see it before you return it to him? No. Let me recite Poonks's poem that he wrote for you when he was seven years old, and see if I miss one word."

Dixie took the poem out from her suitcase, and said, "Recite it, Aunt Ruby."

"Dixie Boom Boom, every word I recite wrongly, I'll give you one hundred dollars. I always keep money in my bra for emergency." Aunt Ruby began: Dixie Boom Boom, you think you cute. You not cute. Cash Nixon is more cute, cute, cute than you is. She let me sit on the swing with her every day. She is fearer than you with her color. She can dance better than you. She wares good closes. But guess something? I love you more, because you is you, And you let me choose first when Aunt Ruby put our food on the table, esspeshlly her fry plantain. From Poonks, your best friend fourever, and fourever, and more fourever. "How many mistakes I made?"

"Only one, Aunt Ruby. You said love. He says like in his poem dedicated to me."

Aunt Ruby went in her bosom and took the money from her bra. "Here's your hundred dollars."

"Aunt Ruby, the way you recited that poem, you stopped my tears. But you purposely made that mistake to pay me from your estate profits. But I will take your money to take Poonks to a movie tonight."

"Take him to see Widows or The Green Book."

"I will let Poonks make his choice."

"Is that your usual habit? You always let the man make the choice."

"Aunt Ruby, you know I always let Poonks choose first."

"That's why you went on the floor and let

him pinch your naked buttocks?" Both of them chuckled. "Dixie, and you keep that habit for all men?"

"Just the men who treat me right—black, brown or white."

"How many are, or were they?"

Dixie looked at her sternly.

"Dixie, this is not a woman asking a child an adult question. We are both women. Ask me the same question, and I'll answer you truthfully."

"I think I'm falling in love slowly with Cocoa Panyol, the older man."

"Is he the one who caused you to slam your cell on the floor? That's an expensive Apple iPhone."

"Yes."

"Don't you think your love for this older man could be infatuation?" She looked at Dixie.

"Yes; it could be, but it is not."

"Go-ahead."

"The man I'd been living with for two years, almost three...." She stopped.

"What happened to that man?"

"I walked out on him in the most unceremoniously way."

"Why?"
"As I told you before, I left him to meet Poonks at JFK Airport, and Poonks was gone. Poonks could have waited to catch the next flight. I was in dirty clothes, sweaty, and I could smell my perspiration. This older man—I prefer to say older, than old—took me in to live free in his three-story brownstone."

"Both of you are copulating?"

"Yes; we are; but I was the aggressor, and I forced myself on him after six plus months living by him. It became living with him as his wife. But he showed no signs of letting me get between his satin sheets in the first six months I have been there."

"Since you are here, Poonks got between your sheets?"

"Not yet?"

"What not yet means?"

"No doubt, he will; and it will be grand. He won't have to peep to see if my breasts are still small or inflated. They will be on his chest."

"Would you be making dinner for Poonks tonight?"

"After movie, I'm taking him to a motel. I will be doing the choosing of the motel, not he."

"My last advice to you is: Uncle Roy and I are old, and everything I own will be given to Poonks in a deed, not a will, before I die; and I will tell him the sum of money I want him to donate to you when I die; but before you go I will give you some of your Juilliard Performing Arts money that you refused by not going to that great school."

Dixie looked at her.

"It will not be a large sum, and I'll be giving it to you in a bank check before you leave. You will also have that naked painting with the man's protruding penis that you admired when you were eight years old. Please, don't get immersed in your own life as a worm in a rotten fruit. Explore, explore, explore. The activism of others and their search for truth can be akin to yours. You will surely see what it means to make difficult choices. Your difficulty is not unique. Poonks, Uncle Roy and I realized a long time that you are in love with someone else." Aunt Ruby went into her drawer, took out her debit card, told her the pin, and said, "Spend as much time in the best hotel, not a motel. Because of you, Poonks is alive today to make me and Uncle Roy plant more roses on this beautiful land that we bought when we left Brooklyn. Take the Mercedes, and don't let Poonks drive because he may be too excited to know he'll be seeing your breasts with your permission, and his excitement may cause him another accident when you are about to go to see the older man and you will not want that to happen. My last words of advice to you, Dixie Boom Boom, are do not shackle your heart to a gone by memory." She hid her smile.

Both were dressed casually, but only Dixie knew where they were finally going. Finally, Jason said, "That's the third movie place you passed. All of them are showing the movies I want to see."

"I prefer you see all the movies by looking at the curves I've developed in my body, all the molds I have, if my breasts are still goats' breasts, if my nipples get harder when your lips touch them, and what happens if I say the ceiling needs painting when we are in bed, and I am on my back, and looking up?"

"Sometimes you'll be on top, so I will see the dirty ceiling. I am not going to a dirty motel."

"So you have taken your white women to dirty motels?"

He didn't answer.

"They fuck good?"
He didn't answer.

"They move their bodies up and down under the dick?"

He didn't answer.

"So you are ready to change places and do as the French people?"

"Cocoa Panyol is from France?"

"No."

"From what country?"

"The Republic of Trinidad and Tobago, the land of calypso. Well, we'll do it the calypsonian way too with cunnilingus galore. I'm going to park. I have a Chase debit card, so you give the valet a big tip."

"Yes, Madame Panyol."

"I want when I go back to CP, every day I live I will be thinking of you because I will never forget what you did for my deceased mother and me."

"Thank you for my poem; it was yours. You embossed it so beautifully, but why is that sad note written in the back of the poem?"

"My mother told me ingratitude is worse than witchcraft."

"You saved my life too. What can I do now?"

"I've brought clothes for the week for both of us. I want you to make love to me every day, every night, vulgar love, before I return to Brooklyn. I told Cocoa Panyol I was coming, but I did not tell him the exact date or time."

"Are you trying to catch him with the French woman in his beautiful brownstone?

Don't answer. How vulgar should my love making be before you return to that old man?"

"Refer to him as an older man, not an old man, and I'll show you how vulgar your sex should be compared to the older man's, whose love making makes me talk gibberish when he's on top of me. You'll like my new experience so much that we'll stay another week competing who is more vulgar in bed—you or the older man."

They stayed three weeks. Their sexual vulgarity everywhere in the rooms was wonderful.

CHAPTER 10

The human story of faults and fears, disappointments and betrayals, joy and loneliness, happiness and sadness, when they are in our courts we find ourselves, sometimes, befuddled as if we are negotiating with running water with lilies in between when it comes to our love affairs and our heart breaks. But soon we find "love liberates" and we move forward with optimism when we think we are no longer the jilted one in the love affair as it was in the past when betrayal was evident. That's how Cocoa Panyol felt when Dixie left—she would in no way jilt him when Jason gets better from his motor accident and Jason's virility is now active. Nevertheless, Cocoa Panyol was negotiating with his feelings: whether this young woman in his life was also negotiating with her feelings towards him.

Suddenly, the phone rang. It was Dixie's voice. "I'm coming home this week."

"When? What airline? Which flight?"

She hung up without answering any questions. Then he remembered he had not read her letter she left hidden in her pillowcase, and she would be indeed furious if on her return she found out he didn't read her letter. She always fluffed their pillows and pulled the sheets so firmly that a penny if fallen on the sheet would bounce off on their beds as if the meticulous Army sergeant would come and make inspections. Sometimes Cocoa Panyol imitated her, made the ritual truly enjoyable, and both would jump on and off the bed saying, "Let's rumple the bed again before the sergeant comes." And they would. But she would say when they had finished their lovemaking on the rumpled sheet, "Panyol, it's your time to make up the bed before the sergeant's inspection; and if ever there's punishment or praise for you, it will be written and placed in my pillowcase."

Not knowing the exact day when Dixie would be coming home, he became vigilant in finding her letter because he never made his bed since she left. As soon as he found her letter in the pillowcase, he was wondering if what is written is his punishment, and what could that punishment be: Could it be because he refused to take her money as rental or money for his water bills because she stays very long in the tub; could it be because she always had to call him upstairs to lie with her, and she waited for more than six months to have sex for the first time, and he wasn't the one who negotiated for them to have fun in bed; could it be because his French girlfriend, Aime, hung up on her, and he objected to how she, Dixie, had called Aime a yellow whore. Aime replied, "We know each other's game."

"Panyol," she had asked then in an argument before she left for Florida, "who's the worse, fuckin ho—the yellow, ho-bitch in Paris who told me we know each other's game or the black, ho-bitch in Brooklyn that you rescued in Uber before you know my game?"

He didn't answer.

"What should I do when next that French ho calls you, her man, and I'm home?"

"No whores call me. My friend, Aime, is a good friend. Our sex life is long over."

"So I'm the only ho you fuckin?"

"Dix, I will never disaffect your self-image." He had hugged her then, and she had apologized, and had said, "Sometimes your imaginary problems bring on your tender emotions. If I have a problem it is I'm not falling in love with you; I am deeply in love with you since I stepped into Uber; and I'm afraid of disappointment. At my age, I'm no longer playing the field. What about you?"

"I'm forty three. What if I'm playing the field today, Panyol?"

"If I were your age, I would have been tracking your every footstep to know if you are a submarining lover, disappearing and then appearing after your pearl got cleaned."

"Are you, at seventy three, the guy who disappears to France, then appears in Brooklyn as an expert in submarining, who comes and smells my pearl before shining it?"

"Those days are over, Dix."

"The ocean is dry for your submarining?"

"Yes."

"Which ocean?"

"All of them."

Then she continued: "For the first two

years I'm with you, you have gone to France three times and you never told me where you were going."

He had looked at her then.

Suddenly his mind came back to the present time and realized he hadn't read Dixie's letter that she had hidden in her pillowcase. He took the letter out of the pillowcase.

It reads: My loving Cocoa Panyol, this letter is long. But, please, read every word, my heart. Let me tell you now so it will be written before I die—not that I am hoping to die now before I return, but death comes without a warning—that I will always love you. I've been asking myself, what is love? Is it something that will make me happy, or make me sad with your explanations? Thus, there are few questions I will want you to answer before I return to you, my love.

As you know, I'm going to give blood to Jason for what he had done for me and my loving mother who is deceased. In my mother's prayers at nights before her death she always asked God to bless Jason—she called him Poonks sometimes—and also Aunt Ruby for their kindness exhibited to us (mother and me) for many years until we were able to go and live on our own. Aunt Ruby handed my mother an envelope, and my mother was shocked to see the amount of money in the envelope when we said goodbye to her. I am telling you this to let you know I would not have packed to go to Florida and leave you if I were not going to repay their good deeds with my humble kindness which is giving my O-negative blood to save Jason which may or may not work.

I also want you to know, no matter what love feelings Jason may develop for me, or what amount of money he puts in my account to encourage me to stay with him or to marry him, I will be returning to your arms, and if you don't want me only then, I will return to Jason, but sadly. Another question is: If I tell you that I was in a temporary sexual affair, and not a love affair, with Jason, would you take me back?

Panyol, in my adult life, I've gone to bed with few men, probably more than a few, sexually; I'd loved them, but I had never fallen in love with them no matter how romantic they were, as I'm not falling in love with you. Truthfully, I have already fallen in love with you, deeply. When I return, if I didn't die in a plane crash or a car crash which is so prevalent these days, should you take me in your brownstone, I will bend on my knees and ask you to marry me. It isn't that I'm afraid you'd return to France to marry your old flame. My only reason for asking you to marry me is my love for you is deep as the ocean, and no woman, young or old, will take care of you when you become older, and probably sick, needing caregiving. I know if I return, you may ask, "Dix, why do you return?" I can't prophesy an answer now, probably only when we go in the tub together. Smile.

I will tell Jason and Aunt Ruby about you. And, for sure, Aunt Ruby will remind me about the old man who wanted to rape me when I was a girl in middle school. Aunt Ruby always gave me a thermos with hot water and a pack of tea to have at recess time. I knew the culture of the people and their uncharitable behavior seeing black people are moving into the neighborhood, and I knew nearly everyone who walked my route to Marine Park Middle School. One morning as I made a shortcut and walked through the Marine Park savannah I saw a man that I'd never seen in the neighborhood before, following me, and knowing Aunt Ruby always taught Jason and me to be offensive is better than being defensive when our life is in danger, I uncapped my thermos. When the man was a hand length away from my back, I turned around quickly, threw the piping-hot water in his face, and he ran away in the opposite direction.

For many days I asked myself if my premeditated act was indeed wrong. But I was not wrong. I saw that man the next day with a bandage on his face stealing an old woman's purse. Am I again not wrong in premeditating that you will be my lover undoubtedly when I return?

In Florida I will remind myself that you have told me there's a choice in our life of whether we are going to laugh or whether we are going to cry and I will go to bed nightly listening to Michael Feinstein singing "Grateful" softly in my ear. I will sing that tune to you when we are in the tub because you are the best thing that ever happened to me. And I'd also tell you sunlight is the greatest insecticide; I had used God's sunlight and my savvy to determine who you are; and I have found you are the only human alive that my heart wants and yearns for every minute of the day.

Goodbye for now, my love. I can't wait to return to hug my Cocoa Panyol under the satin sheets to rejoice, sing, and jubilate because of what you will be doing to my body and my pearl as only you in my adult life cause me to have that feeling, and to tell you I love you even in a whisper when I lose my voice because of a mishap. If you couldn't hear me when I lose my voice, but you can only see my eyes for one second, my eyes will be telling you I love you before I close them and never open them again. Sadly, but that's true.

Remember I am Dix, who teaches you bedtime tricks better than Frenchie ever did even when she was young, and now that she is older, she's a minus in bed compared to me. Smile. Invite her when we are married to our home, and let us be friends so we can have French fries as our welcome dish for our friendship, and I know she will laugh out loud as if she's mocking that someone she knows in the White House who lies faster that a horse trots, and who says he is the Chosen One and the King of Israel. Honey, I love you so much. We have one life, and we should live it with integrity is my only advice to you, ole man, who shares my space in bed.

Meeting you was a red-letter day that I'll never forget in my lifetime. I'm going to repeat myself but I will say it again: I love you so much, and I'm asking you, please, to marry me. If you die before me, I'll take your blood to improve the texture of my skin. Would you, please, Cocoa Panyol, put my request in your last will and testament?

See you soon, my love,
Dix Waltz Dunkirk

He rested her letter on the loveseat on

which they watched TV for she would see the letter and would be happy to know he read it. He cried aloud, and said, "Dix, I will marry you. Dix, I'd marry you. Dix, I'd marry you. I didn't ask you before because I thought you'd marry Poonks to repay his kindness to you and your mother."

He changed his mind from going to France to settle on a property that Aime was negotiating the right price for them. He was doing this business unknown to Dixie to surprise her, but he was one hundred percent sure Dixie would not believe him; so his intention was as soon as she returns from Florida he would take her to France to see Aime, and to hear of what Aime was doing for them.

Cocoa Panyol sat down, his tears dripped, and he replied to Dixie Waltz Dunkirk's letter:

Dix, my only love, I think of us as the enrichment couple because we have already put the do's and don'ts of our friendship at the fore of our memory, and we have weighed all the mishaps and normal problems that have faced us since we met in Uber. Meeting you, I have learned how to disagree in love. I have never been able to do that with other lovers. I look forward to the summer months when our lives buzz with activity. On the Amtrak traveling home from seeing my daughter and grandchildren who live in North East, Maryland, to returning home to be with you, I see glimpses of America passing by when I look through the window. I gaze at the little towns with their farm lands and animals grazing, the vast expanse of water, the bridges, the wide roads, some standing on steel stilts just as in my loving New York, New York, and then my mind runs on you and what are you doing in Florida.

Dix, as you know, I am thirty years your senior, but an examination of life tells me you will be my wife for the rest of my life. The very thought of you has my tears dripping on my computer, but I will continue to write this letter because my heart and soul desire you by remembering Thanksgiving is celebrating the day Americans, the Indians, fed the undocumented expatriates from Europe. Equally true, Thanksgiving is when you fed me with your untarnished love and said love has no limit on age. On your flight from Florida to sweet Brooklyn I will be thinking of you from the minute you step in the plane for I know when you return home our lush life will start afresh. If I'm dedicated to you it is because you are my stairway to the stars because you show me love is grand when I am with you, and I also see my Thanksgiving in you with your gifts of love for me. In the early morning when the sun is bright in the eastern room, and I sleep there now in your absence to smell your sweet body odor on your pillow, my imagination takes me to places, but knowing you will be coming home to me my imagination becomes reality knowing we will be between the satin sheets—and I bought two new ones because I like your rhythm under them as windmills moving with the wind, clockwise and counterclockwise—and I will again imagine that I'm in La Trinidad on the cocoa trees sucking the sweet pods of cocoa. But it will not be my imagination for it will be your pods that my palate will be enjoying when you return.

We will have group therapy and that therapy will be making love to each other; we will not be two dolphins in a shark tank, but two dolphins with other dolphins climbing on each other showing all the world needs is love. Every night I will kiss you when you are asleep because I know your subconscious thoughts are never asleep and it will tell you I kissed you because my love is ineffable for words. Once I emptied my ear ducts when I listened to other jilted lovers, and, sometimes, adjudicated their disagreements, and I say, glibly, romance is a game for fools. I now say romance is made for you and me. We are sensible fools because we know we love each other and we have a permanent crush on each other, and though we pretend sometimes that it isn't so, we now know we are agents of change in our own life. We are *pari passu*, on equal grounds, in our sexual desires, not holding back our emotions between the satin sheets that you had bought for my birthday. When you gave those sheets to me for my first birthday with you, and I had asked you could Frenchie come between them with us, your laughter was so loud that all the neighbors on Greene Avenue knew that we did it good, whether with rain on the roof making music, whether with the sunlight coming through the eastern windows, and whether with the snow blinding our vision as we look through the windows. And they were right.

My past is a prologue, that behavior that led to situation after situation that militated against my sensibility, but today I will not look once more in the mirror and tell myself it is a window. I did that once, got jilted in love, and told myself never would I be such a fool again. When Marie Antoinette, the last Queen of France before the French Revolution, being told her French peasants need bread, she sniffed, "Let them eat cake." When being told by beautiful women, "Cocoa Panyol, you are equally a stupid ignoramus as that French woman who didn't know what her peasants meant when they said they need bread, you are a similar fool who doesn't know what my body needs even when it is naked in front of you." I always reply to them, "I'd eat Antoinette's cake instead of yours." Dix, ask me the same question when you come home to see how ravenously I'd suck your pods.

Dix, your returning home is proof that it is not the end of our love affair but the confirmation of our oneness in love till death. And I believe more than ever when you said being forty three in the sunrise years of your life you will be around for my sunset. I am anxiously awaiting your arrival. I know I cannot do great things but I will do small things in a great way for you. The greatest things in life are not things but someone as you—that special someone I found in Uber. Meeting you was a gold-star moment. My uxorious habit of kissing you before you go into the car and blowing a kiss when you leave earned me a teasing by the neighbors, and I love that teasing.

Who knows I may be on the stoop waiting for you, my only love.

John "Cocoa Panyol" Dinkins.

CHAPTER 11

Florida was extremely hot in Citrus Springs; the sun's rays found Aunt Ruby's pool and gave it a temperature that made swimming comfortable for the naked bodies. The landscape that enveloped the pool had flowers of every hue that were planted by Uncle Roy. Uncle Roy, as smart as a fox, said, "Ruby, let's go to the estate and see what the men are doing. Trucks should be coming today for oranges." Ruby knew why Roy wanted her to leave the house, and she said, "Okay, Roy. I'll cook a quick pot to take with us, and then we'll leave for the day." Both spoke loud enough for Jason and Dixie who were sitting by the swimming pool to hear.

Ruby shouted, "Poonks and Dixie Boom Boom, don't leave the house to buy street food. I've cooked good, Jamaican food, food that hits the ribs for days, and you can lick your fingers for days after you eat. You don't even have to put your dirty dishes in the dishwasher after you eat."

Dixie said, "Aunt Ruby, don't forget I'm leaving on the 3 pm flight to New York today."

"I'm doing business today, so I can tell you goodbye from now. You don't know how I cried when you left me to go and live on your own, and you did not give me your address. I am not coming back before you leave to cry a second time around."

"Aunt Ruby, I regretted what I did, but I am inviting you, Uncle Roy, and Poonks, to visit me in Brooklyn. There is enough room to house all of you, and privately. Would you come, Aunt Ruby?"

"Sure, I want to see what Cocoa Panyol looks like. I will open Cocoa Panyol's vault to see if that French woman is hiding in it. I don't trust any man whom I don't know his culture. I will not be leaving my common sense that I've acquired over the years at the JFK airport. You may, or may not, know I love you as much as I love Poonks. Safe travel home; don't come close to me to kiss me. My last advice to you is: don't shackle your heart to a bygone memory. Let Cocoa Panyol be the one. I end my speech."

"Uncle Roy, would you come too?"

"That's the first invitation I get to come back to my Brooklyn since I left that carefree place twenty years ago. I'd love to come for you to take me to Harlem to see the re-gentrification, and to go to the Apollo. I heard President Clifton has an office there."

Jason said yes, softly, to Dixie's invitation.

Aunt Ruby said, "Speak louder Poonks. What do you say?"

"I'd be there to ask that old man..."

Dixie interrupted him, "Older man."

"I will be there to ask that older man, why it is him and not me...."

Aunt Ruby shouted, "Poonks, no Ebonics in front of me today."

"Why it is he, and it is not I," Jason corrected his grammar. "Aunt Ruby, it is time to leave for your estate so that I can practice my Ebonics on Dixie Boom Boom."

"Is that the only thing you want to practice on her in my and Uncle Roy's absence?"

Their loud laughter was heard in the quiet surrounding. Aunt Ruby and Uncle Roy walked to the car with two bags with their lunch without saying goodbye to Dixie, and Dixie knew why. She too remembered how Aunt Ruby wept, and how Uncle Roy lifted her bodily back into their Brooklyn home. Whenever Roy drove off, he usually toots his horn. He didn't, but Dixie run from the pool and looked at their Mercedes Benz meander through the winding roads until she could see it no more. But this time she was the one who cried a river.

Jason took her in his arms, led her to the loveseat, used his still hurting arms and rested her down softly. But she saw he was in pain.

"Poonks, I know how that pain could end?"

"How?"

"Swimming in our birthday suits."

"Okay. But let's eat what Aunt Ruby cooked first. Dish out my lunch for the last time before you go to that older man. Did I use the correct adjective?"

"Yes, Poonks; you did."

"And when we go swimming naked, would I get some loving dolphins' behavior?"

"What's loving dolphins' behavior?"

"After we eat, and I lead you to the pool, I will show you loving dolphins' behavior."

"Would you be climbing the cocoa tree, picking the cocoa, opening it, and sucking the sweet pods?"

"Who does that?"

"Cocoa Panyol."

"He uses his palate because his dick is dead."

"Well, I will be judging your stamina and comparing his palate's prowess with your dick."

"I'm still an out-patient at Michael Bilirakis DVA Spinal Cord Injury Center at James A. Harley Veterans' Hospital in Tampa."

"I'm going to Brooklyn. I will not be going there to that Veterans' hospital if you try to better Panyol's stamina in the pool today. My O-negative blood is for Cocoa Panyol if he needs it in his older years."

“I’m laughing but I’m getting jealous, Dixie Boom Boom.”

“In the hotel, you showed me you do it better when you are jealous. In water, I want to see if you are just as good as Cocoa Panyol, a descendant of the First Peoples. He does it in the tub, and I love the way he does it.”

“I’m over with your stupid diatribe.”

“Why over? Poonks, it’s you who started the competition with yourself. This may be the last time that I’m telling you how grateful I am for saying, Ask Aunt Ruby; she helps everybody. Having sex with you is to say goodbye for now, not always, but it is not a payment for a debt I owed; it is saying to you I love you with sex, without using words.”

“Isn’t that like eating without enjoying what you are eating?”

“Are you telling me you don’t want to go naked in the pool again, but you prefer to go and play love songs on the piano? I never knew you can play so beautifully. I remember as children, I played better than you, and Aunt Ruby had to force you to play. How come you left ball playing and went to the upright piano?”

"I was in love with a lovely teenager, and I knew my ball playing ability was the worst compared to the other boys who tried to court her."

"Do I know who that teenager is?"

"Yes."

"Who?"

"You. And then you left me by Aunt Ruby, went on your own, and left no address that I could find you. To remember you, I played love songs to you imagining you were sitting next to me on the piano stool. I played every night, *For All We Know We May Never Meet Again.*"

"I will play it for you this time. Whenever I play that song in the food court, the girls always ask if I'm playing that song for Jason or Darwin."

"Who is Darwin?"

"Didn't I tell you he is the man I left unceremoniously when I lost your flight?"

"Where was the older man then?"

"I didn't even know him."

"So you can still tickle the ivory keys? Why you never played for Aunt Ruby and Uncle Roy to hear you?"

"You know what Aunt Ruby's swansong would be: 'I worked hard like hell and saved my money to send Poonks to be an engineer, and he became one; and, you, Dixie Boom Boom, I wanted to send you to Juilliard's, the Performing Arts College to be a concert pianist, and you walked away not leaving an address where we could find you.' Don't you think I remember how stupid I was to lose that opportunity? All I do now is to write in my newspaper what Putin Trump, Moscow Mitch, Doonbeg Pence, the Secretary of State, Attorney General Bill Barr and their money-and-power-grabbing friends do to for themselves and not for their country. And they lie about not having knowledge about Ukraine's scandal which they participated in. Such liars! Nevertheless, Trump got impeached. You don't have to believe me but there's a keyboard in the food court where I work, and I go and play couple tunes when I become stressed thinking of you. Cocoa Panyol wanted to buy a grand piano for me, but I told him not to. I was afraid I would have been thinking of you when I play."

He looked at her.

“True.” She looked at him too. “And, please, don’t play *Young and Foolish* when I’m leaving for me to bawl down this place and chase all the animals from their habitats in Citrus Springs. Lest I forget, I don’t want you to drive me to the airport. I’ll call Uber.”

“I wasn’t taking you, and that’s final. Let’s go skin diving so I can give it to you under water.”

“I’d like that. But help me eat some of this fried plantain and those other cooked food, and I will help you eat some of your callalloo. But don’t touch my meat.”

“I won’t touch the meat in your plate that Aunt Ruby cooked. I know what meat to touch.”

Dixie smiled. “Did you touch the meat of the woman you brought to Bobby’s birthday party or those you brought to your room here? You don’t have to answer.”

He smiled.

“Is that a yes or a no?”

He laughed and threw food on her.
They became children again. They threw

food at each other, picked up food from the floor and forced it into each other's mouth. They drank from one glass, pretended they spat in the glass, handed the glass to each other, and each drank as if spit were nectar. The place was very dirty, and, suddenly, Jason shouted, "I heard a car in the driveway." He peeped, and said softly, "It is Aunt Jan, Uncle Reggie, and their daughter, Nicky. If they ring the bell one thousand times, don't answer."

"The way I want to make love to you before getting on my flight, I will never answer if they ring the bell two thousand times. This will be the last hours of my lush life in the pool so nothing or anybody will spoil it knowing you'll soon be covering the waterfront."

They enjoyed their lovemaking in the pool, and at the end of their romance, both of them cried, each saying as they embraced, "I'll miss you, Poonks."

"I'll miss you, Dixie Boom Boom. Before you leave, go on the piano and play something for me."

"Like what?"

"Anything."

She began playing *For All We Know We May Never Meet* and a medley of songs, but when she switched to *I Only Have Eyes For You*, Poonks, he couldn't stop crying, and he said, "Call Uber now. I'm not taking you to the airport."

"Why, Poonks?"

"With the tears in my eyes, I won't be able to see the road, and I'll surely get into another motor vehicle accident with you, and probably both of us will die. Don't even say goodbye when your ride comes. Just leave."

"Here."

He took an envelope from her hand; he rested it on the table, but he didn't look to see what was in the envelope. It was a portrait of them sitting on the step of Aunt Ruby's house in Brooklyn with the two Italian-American racists in the background.

The flight to JFK was delayed, and she went looking for things to buy to kill time and the thought of Poonks and her as children was vivid in her mind. She wanted to call him, but she fought against herself and won. She turned off her cell because she felt if he called her she'd return and may never leave his arms, remembering the way he cried when she put his name to the song, *I Only Have Eyes For You*, Jason.

When she boarded the plane, she turned on her cell and waited on a call from him, but he did not call her. She turned off her cell again, spoke to herself and said, If he were interested in me he would have called. She listened to the flight attendant's instructions, turned off the light overhead, and went to bed. When she got up from her two-plus-hours sleep, she looked through the window, and, instinctively, she knew she was over Queens, New York. She discerned Interstate 678, a north-south auxiliary Interstate Highway that extends through two boroughs of New York City; and the water in Jamaica Bay looked blacker than she saw it before in her many flights back to New York. She only had a light, carry-on luggage, and it was under the seat in front of her. The clothes she brought to Florida and bought in Florida, she left them behind for Aunt Ruby to donate to the needy.

Having not to wait for arriving luggage, she told herself she'll run for a yellow cab to kill time instead of calling Uber as soon as the plane stops taxiing and finally stops. She closed her eyes and was thinking where would Cocoa Panyol be when she arrives. She purposely did not tell him the exact day she was arriving because she knew he'd be cooking her favorite meals, which are many, and if she didn't like the meals he cooked, he'd suggest another to suit her taste at that hour. She did not want to put him in that quandary. She had other plans, many plans; but she could not decide which plan because she was landing on his seventy fourth birthday.

She spoke to herself: When I land I will call a hotel and book two nights, probably three. She looked at the bank check Aunt Ruby slipped in her purse when she was not looking, and she mumbled the words on the memo of the check, Leftover from Juilliard's. Tears flooded her eyes, "Aunt Ruby, I don't need twenty thousand of your hard-earned money." She became silent but her tears dripped endlessly.

The plane was making rounds over JFK. Dixie asked the flight attendant who chatted with her before, why was she seeing the same view below for the last fifteen minutes. "Dixie, the pilot is waiting on the air controllers to tell him on what runway is free to land."

"Thanks, Marie-Sophie. I remember you telling me you are French, and I like France. I wanted to wear your uniform, but I didn't get the job." Dixie closed her eyes and wondered if the landing would be safe, if New York's weather would be the same seventy four degrees as the pilot had said earlier; and, if so, the number 74 will coincide with Cocoa Panyol's age. She whispered, "That's good news. I'll buy two Mega lottos, Take 7, and Take 4. When I win, I will buy a house in France for Cocoa Panyol and me to spend our winters."

The pilot announced they are landing and repeated the temperature is seventy four degrees. She took out her compact and made herself pretty. She stood, and she walked to the front of the plane. "Dixie, I see you are ready to disembark first. Good luck." "Marie-Sophie, say it twice." "Good luck, good luck, Dixie."

Dixie rushed off. The escalators and elevators were too slow for her. She ran through all the exits. Taxis were waiting in line, and passengers had to wait on their turn. Her turn came, and she jumped into the taxi.

"Where to, Miss?"

"Greene Avenue, the number is on my business card. Hold it."

"Where are you coming from?"

"Florida."

"You like Florida?"

“Yes.”

To me, flat Florida without mountains, is like a beautiful woman without breasts.”

‘That’s your subjective views, not mine.”

“So you were away from New York’s politics?”

“I was away from it, but I’m going back to be head deep in it because I was away and was not listening.”

“You heard Trump went to North Korea and came back empty handed? And he told the four, black American Congresswomen to go back to the infested country they came from?”

“Not really.”

“You heard he said 817 Fake News were mentioned about him, and he told twelve thousand plus lies in his 936 days in office.”

“Not really.”

“But I’m sure you heard his fixer, Michael Cohen, exposed his allegedly criminal enterprise?”

"Not really."

"Didn't you hear Trump's lawyer in crime, say Trump is a racist, a con man, and a thief?"

"Not really."

"And you also didn't hear Michael Cohen accuses Trump of bank fraud, insurance fraud, tax evasion, and suborning perjury."

"Not really."

"Did you see the checks Trump cut for his fixer to pay for a criminal purpose?"

"Not really."

"Have you not been following how Trump held back the money Congress passed for Ukraine to fight Russia until Ukraine give him dirt on his political opponent?"

"Not really. Where did you go to school?"

"Why are you asking me where did I go to school? You think because I drive a taxi, I am not smart enough to give me an answer, except not really. Where you stayed in Florida, there is no TV?"

"Yes, a TV is in every room; it is a very big house."

"And you didn't listen to the news? I'm from South Africa, and I remember Nelson Mandela saying, 'Fools multiply when wise men are silent.' The Congress and the Senate are silent about Trump's ocean-full of twelve thousand plus lies, and fools are multiplying daily seconding Trump's lies. How come you have not been hearing these things?"

"I didn't care to listen because before I left for Florida Michael Cohen flipped because he got caught. When thieves fall out honest men get their due. I spent my valuable time crying over the end of a love affair in Citrus Springs, Florida."

"You alone were crying?"

"No; both of us."

"And why didn't you remain and mend the broken love affair? Didn't you hear Peggy Lee sing, *Don't Cry. There'll Be Another Spring*? Sometimes we have to pick a road in the woods; and only when it is dark you can see the stars."

"I wanted to move on."

"Good luck."

"What's a good birthday gift for a man?"

"For me? My birthday is next week."

They laughed.

"For a kind man."

"How old?"

"Seventy four years old today."

"Your grandfather?"

"No."

"Who?"

"The man I'm going to marry, if he still wants me."

"He's rich?"

"Rich in character. If I'm lucky, I'll go through the years with him."

"What about in sex?"

"Don't you think you are getting too personal?"

"I'm very sorry, Miss. Please, forgive my impertinence. But let me talk about myself now, if you will listen and give me some advice, except not really."

"Yes, I'll listen."

"I'm paying for a child in court in this United States of America, and I'm one hundred percent sure that is not my child."

"How do you know that?"

"I am black in race and in skin color. That child was born white, but I thought his complexion would change to brown because his mother is brown. The child is five and he is still very white with blue eyes."

"I don't know what to tell you, but, for sure, I know you have to stop now because I live in the brownstone that you are approaching as you turn. Here's your fee and a tip for your safe driving, for informing me about New York politics, and about the Radical in Chief's lies. If Obama had done one-hundredth of what that liar whose syntax is horrendous, Obama would have been impeached or serving time in jail." She handed him a tip after she paid.

He looked at the money, and shouted, "Thank you! Thank you! Here's my business card. If you need a taxi to take you back to the airport to go back to Florida if the old man you are going to meet today is no good in bed, call me to take you back to Florida to meet the young man."

"The old man is my heart, in and out of bed. Black man, you have a child with blue eyes because you thought you were good in bed. The other, John Public, was plenty better. My advice to you is to maintain your child, and he'll take care of you in your old age."

"I'll take your advice. Thanks again for the big tip. Have a joyous wedding with your folks dancing the electric slide."

"You described our racist President's macabre compulsion very well. You should go into politics."

"Would you join me?"

"Only if the old man wants me to."

"Bring your grandpa to join my political party. Old people have money, and your old man will contribute with plenty green paper. No checks!"

"If I do, he will tell the world that Trump, the man-child, got caught listening to a man named Giuliani who says 'truth is not truth,' and Trump held back the money for Ukraine abusing the power of his office for personal gains, and he was impeached on December 18, 2019 because there was *quid pro quo*."

"So you were listening to the weaponized news?"

"And what is worst of all is that since January 2020 and probably before members of his Intelligence Service had been warning him about the Coronavirus pandemic and what the serious consequences would be to mankind. He ignored them, and kept the knowledge of this virus pandemic away from the public. That's a criminal act. A prestigious newspaper writes, 'Donald Trump has blood on his hands.' And I agree. Now he goes on the TV and America hears his stentorian voice of lies. Did you know that?"

"Not really."

"But you surely know he's telling us to inject ourselves with disinfectant to kill the virus in our lungs?"

"Not really."

"Stop that not really bullshit."

"You started it."

"Now my bullshit is ended! Let yours end too. Yesterday the Columbia Study stated on March 8, 2020, if Trump had paid attention to what is taking place and did what he was advised to do to fight the blow of the Coronavirus pandemic, 36,000 lives would have been saved. But he was playing golf with his kith and kin on that day. What do you say?"

"My heart is saddened to the core knowing your racist President's thinking is like 'an archipelago of dots.'"

"Since you have a heart, my bridegroom and I will invite you to our wedding, and we will join your political party."

Both of them laughed aloud. Their voices were heard on Nostrand Avenue, the eastern end of the block.

"One more thing, my friend."

"What, madam bride-to-be?"

"What should be done to that Minneapolis white Police Officer Derek Chauvin who put his murderous knee on black George Floyd's neck for eight minutes and forty six seconds and killed him?"

"If I tell you what I'll cut off with the shears I keep in my car, you will lose your concentration crossing the street."

"Not really!"

"What about if I tell you what I will shave off those other three bastards who watched while Chauvin with his hand in his pocket casually killed Floyd?

"Not really."

Both laughed as loud as Florida's thunder.

CHAPTER 12

For the whole day Cocoa Panyol was immobile. He sat on the step and talked to his neighbors and made jokes with them as they walked by. He was popular in the neighborhood.

Dixie stepped out of the right side of the cab laughing joyously at her conversation with the cabby. Another vehicle parked on the same side of the street blocked her view of approaching vehicles as she crossed the street and walked to her gate. Still laughing, she lost her concentration when someone who knows her, saw her, as he was walking down his steps; and he shouted excitedly, "Dix! Dix! Dix! I cooked crab and deep fried rolls with onion soup for you."

She heard that familiar voice, and shouted louder, "Cocoa Panyol, that's my favorite food. I love you! I love you! I bought a gift for you." She dropped her hand luggage, rushed across the street looking neither left nor right, up nor down.

Cocoa Panyol screamed, "Dix, no! no!"

His screams were too late. A speeding car driving east on Greene Avenue trying to evade the police siren for him to stop, knocked her flush into the air almost five yards ahead. She fell bodily on her face and her blood gushed freely.

When Cocoa Panyol picked her up, his hands and clothes bloodied, her eyes opened and closed immediately. He pulled her eye lids apart, opened them to see her eyes, but death was already evident. He hugged her dead body, her blood painted his body, flowed over his nose and on to his lips. He never let her go, only when the police came. But he was saying over and over again, "I was going to marry you, Dix. I love you, Dix, you are dead, but I will send you roses to mark our anniversary of our meeting in Uber." He screamed aloud, nonstop.

The police came and investigated what took place and, finally, an ambulance drove her body to the mortuary.

A hand touched him. "I am Officer Kirl

Cardus from Precinct 71. What's your name?"

"My legal name is John Pitkins, but my friends call me Cocoa Panyol. Officer Cardus, you can call me that too."

"Cocoa Panyol, I'm here to help you."

"Officer, I have a gun upstairs. I will show you where I hid it. I will shoot myself through the heart if you don't take my gun."

"Panyol, don't waste your tomorrow by an unnecessary act today. Don't let the afternoon be a Romeo and Juliet's moment. Let it be an Anna Karenina's evening. Live to see your grandchildren grow to lengthen posterity so your memory will never die. Go upstairs and call Dixie's family. Think, Cocoa Panyol. It may be a new experience in your life, and wisdom will whisper in your ear. Be wise, my friend. No one can escape the vicissitudes of life, and we all must adapt to the changes they bring. Danielle Steel says it best: It is the hard stuff that makes us what we are."

"Officer Cardus, like Dorothy in the Wizard of Oz, she wanted to get back to Kansas, but she didn't know how."

"Cocoa Panyol, you told me in our long

conversation Dix loved you as no one did; she is back to Brooklyn, but she's dead. Don't forget to send her roses on the anniversary of when both of you first met. Go inside and cry as long as you wish, look for her love letters and read them over and over."

Officer Cardus held his both shoulders firmly and kept looking into his eyes. Cocoa Panyol stopped screaming, but he was still crying. Officer Cardus braced him firmly, spoke softly in his ear, and left.

Cocoa Panyol went upstairs, read and reread Dixie's letter, especially the lines, Cocoa Panyol, I love you so much. I will take your blood to improve my skin, if you will give me. If I'm lucky, I will go through the years with you. He picked up his cell to call someone, cried, and put down his cell. He read her letter again, stopped crying, and called.

"Hello. Who is this? Speak louder. I can't hear you. Are you crying?"

"Yes."

"Who are you?"

"I am John Pitkins, but Dixie Waltz Dunkirk called me Cocoa Panyol."

"Cocoa Panyol, I heard about you from Dixie Boom Boom. She's the daughter I never had. Why are you calling me?"

"Dixie Boom Boom is dead." He dropped his phone, and he wouldn't pick it up.

"Hello, hello! Pick up the blasted phone! Poonks, here's the phone. See if you can hear what that fool is saying."

"Hello. I am Jason. Where is Dixie Boom Boom?"

"She died?"

"When?"

"About three hours ago."

"How come?"

"A car killed her."

"How?"

"When she crossed the street to meet me."

"She just saved my life with her blood. I was in a car accident too."

"She told me about your happy and loving lives together from childhood."

"My Aunt Ruby and I will fly to New York tomorrow."

"Please, do not go to a hotel. I have two empty floors where you and your aunt can stay. I also have a letter Dixie Boom Boom addressed to you when she lost her flight to meet you and to get married to you."

"She died because of me. Had I waited on her, she'd be alive. I need to die too for selfishly only thinking of me getting a new job, and not waiting for her to travel with me."

"God knows best, Jason."

"Thank you, Cocoa Panyol, for your willingness to accommodate us. Dixie Boom Boom was too beautiful for one man alone."

"Poonks, you are telling me God took her for Himself?"

"I don't have that answer."

"Who has that answer, Poonks?"

"Cocoa Panyol, you even know my nickname, as I know yours. Dixie once told me we live on a boulevard of broken dreams. I'm passing the phone to Aunt Ruby. The phone is on speaker. She is listening to us."

"Cocoa Panyol, thanks for your offer; but I've already booked in a hotel. Were you married to Dixie?" Aunt Ruby asked.

"No, but we were going to be married as soon as she returned."

"I will be taking her body to Florida to be buried in the family plot."

"I have already made arrangements to bury her in Cypress Hill, Brooklyn, where my first wife is buried."

"John Pitkins, how dare you! I will never bury her in Brooklyn. Because of you she died in Brooklyn. In Dixie's purse you will see a bank check from me written to Dixie Waltz Dunkirk for twenty thousand dollars. That's her money, so I will use her money to bury her in style. You have been sending your money to buy a property for your woman in France...."

He interrupted her. "Aunt Ruby...."

"I am not your aunt! You are almost my

age. My name is Mrs. Ruby Millicent Argat."

"Mrs. Argat, Dixie knows only the French she learned in college. She doesn't know street French. She translates the subjunctive wrongly. I was buying a property in France for Dixie Waltz Dunkirk and me. My friend, Aime, was the middleman."

"You can buy the property for that mistress of yours. Don't you prefer to do that that, Mr. Pitkins?"

He did not answer.

"Make sure you give me what name you want me to write on her headstone. Do you prefer John Pitkins or Cocoa Panyol?"

"I thank you for that honor, Mrs. Argat. I prefer the name Cocoa Panyol. Would you, please, Mrs. Argat, stay by me when you come to make arrangements to take Dix's body back to Florida?"

She didn't answer. "Would you like to be a pallbearer?"

"That would be one of the greatest gifts of my lifetime."

She became silent and handed the phone to Jason.

"Cocoa Panyol, Aunt Ruby is crying. She likes you. She knows people and their attitudes, and she knows you are a good and kind person. We will be staying by you. Dixie was a wonderful pianist. With your wealth, why didn't you buy a grand piano for her?"

"She said it would be too cumbersome, but I didn't believe her. I'm sure you know the reason why, Poonks?" He didn't answer. "She didn't want a piano in the house because with every note she played she would be remembering you since you were five years old and she was eight."

Jason was silent.

"Jason, don't pretend you didn't hear what I said."

"I am tired, Cocoa Panyol. Her funeral will be a sad, but a grand affair for both of us, pallbearers. Good night, Cocoa Panyol."

"Good night, Poonks. Weeping will endure for the night but joy cometh in the morning."

Aunt Ruby shouted, "For all of us, the

psalmist writes." Their phones were on speaker, and she shouted, "Poonks, hand me that phone." He handed her the phone. "Both of you have shared Dixie's joys and physicality; and when she had whispered her wisdom to both you in the past, I hope both of you had listened. Now that she is gone, think, for it may be a new experience for both of you. Cocoa Panyol, you will read the obituary composed by my husband, you, and me; and Poonks, you will write and read the eulogy because you are the one who introduced Dixie Boom Boom to our home. Do both of you agree to my suggestion?"

"Yes, Aunt Ruby," Poonks said.

"Mrs. Argat, I thank you to be given such an honorable task," Cocoa Panyol said.

"Good night, Cocoa Panyol. I'll be your guest when I come to Brooklyn to make arrangements for her funeral."

"Thank you, Mrs. Argat...." He paused when she whispered something inaudibly.

"It's about time you call me Aunt Ruby."

"Thank you, Aunt Ruby. Good night to you and Poonks."

"Not yet! Boys, before you swap your life story with each other in secret, bend your heads in prayer. Dear Lord, you made us perfectly designed to get through any situation. Before we make a move, before we make a step, before we say a word, we give ourselves to You, and Your guidance, dear Lord. Please, let Your will be done in our lives today in Jesus' holy name. And, Dear Lord, welcome Dixie Waltz Dunkirk into your kingdom. Amen."

"Amen," Cocoa Panyol chorused alone.

Poonks didn't join their chorus, but he took his time to address his aunt. "Aunt Ruby, please, try and remember what I'm saying now: When Dixie Boom Boom refused to go to her prom in the limousine you hired, she took the crosstown B3 bus instead; when she refused to wear the lovely dress you bought for her to graduate from high school, and she wore her dirty, patched jeans which she half covered with her gown, and she refused to go to The Juilliard School of Performing Arts, you said, 'If it is the last thing I'd do, if Dixie Boom Boom dies before me, is to advise God if He sees Dixie Boom Boom coming near to His big House in heaven, He should lock all His doors and run like hell and hide.' Aunt Ruby, you didn't include that in your obituary that you will be delivering tomorrow."

"My dear Poonks, I hope you will include in your eulogy tomorrow how you used to peep at Dixie Boom Boom whenever she was showering in the bathroom and how you purposely cut holes in the shower curtain to have a good look at her pubic hairs; and don't forget to also include in your eulogy the code name, Sergeant Jamaica, you and she called me when both of you were inventing mischief and you and she saw me approaching."

Their boisterous laughter lasted for more than fifteen minutes. Then they said goodnight in unison and laughed even louder again before they hung up.

The funeral in Florida, though tearful, was a very joyous occasion with countless friends and families who enjoyed the elaborate repast prepared by the hands of Aunt Ruby, Uncle Roy, Jason, and Cocoa Panyol.

Cocoa Panyol spent two days at Aunt Ruby and Uncle Roy's beautiful home before returning to Brooklyn. Driving to his home from JFK Airport his ear was plugged listening to Michael Feinstein singing *This Heart of Mine* on his cell phone. That was the last song Dixie and he listened to at bedtime. Alexa obliged.

THE AUTHOR

LLOYD HOLLIS CROOKS was born in Fyzabad, a little oil town, pregnant with political history, in the Republic of Trinidad and Tobago, West Indies. He attended Oxford Commercial College and Medgar Evers College.

In the Republic of Trinidad and Tobago (T&T), Crooks was employed as a Court Reporter, Hansard (Parliament) Reporter, and a Confidential Secretary in Whitehall, the seat of Government, in the Office of the Prime Minister, where he covered "sensitive" national and international conferences. To name one International Conference: The United States of America (USA) and The Republic of Trinidad and Tobago (T&T) Leased Bases Agreement. In that Agreement, in 1963, USA returned to T&T the base leased to them (USA) for 99 years.

In New York, he was a legal assistant to a partner in a prestigious Wall Street law firm. His writing style "narrates a rare eloquence," and, believe me, when reading his novels you become one of the round characters. Crooks lives in Brooklyn, New York, and he lectured at five CUNY Colleges.

Crooks's books and Kindle Edition can be obtained on Amazon. Website: lloydholliscrooks.com

www.ingramcontent.com/pod-product-compliance
Lightning Source LLC
LaVergne TN
LVHW020533100826
845148LV00010B/1440
* 9 7 8 0 5 7 8 6 3 4 1 3 5 *